COYOTE JUNCTION

A Novella

GINGER MARIN

&

J BARTELL

Library of Congress cataloging-in–publication Data has been applied for.
ISBN 979-8-9855122-1-2

Book Design by Bijou Entertainment
Cover Design by Jeanine Henning

DEDICATION

This book is dedicated to Artemis, Cody and Dancer.

CONTENTS

CHAPTER ONE

SINS OF THE SON

The sharp, staccato sound of liquid splattering on the floor echoed faintly through the kitchen, barely audible over the tumultuous clash between Gael Fernandez, a hulking man with muscles that seemed to strain against his skin, and his teenage son. The light from the overhead lamp glinted off Gael's sweat-slicked skin, highlighting the tension in his powerful frame.

Arnold shrank beneath his father's imposing shadow, fear etched on his face, as Gael wielded a thick leather belt menacingly, the veins pulsing angrily in his neck like coiled ropes. But what suddenly seized Arnold's attention more than anything was the gleam of a turquoise eye staring back at him from the belt's ornate metal buckle — a finely detailed hawk, its wings outstretched, burning itself into his memory in that single frozen moment of fear.

The oppressive threat of physical punishment loomed heavily in the air as Gael halted mere inches from striking his son. Instead, he pinned Arnold against the refrigerator with an iron grip, causing a cascade of magnets to crash to the floor while papers fluttered around the room like confetti.

Nearby, a carton of milk lay upended on the kitchen table, its creamy contents spilling forth in a small river that meandered across the surface and dripped steadily towards the floor, adding to the disarray that mirrored the tension in the room.

Alicia, the boy's grandmother, heard the commotion and rushed in, her heart pounding with urgency. She nearly slipped on the slick puddle of spilled milk that glistened on the floor. From beneath the table, a small hand stretched out toward her, trembling and desperate. It belonged to her crying granddaughter, Victoria, who sobbed and screamed, "Grandma!" Her voice was a high-pitched wail, full of fear and pleading.

Alicia struggled to separate Gael from Arnold, her hands shaking with the effort, while Arnold's nine-year-old brother, Frankie, darted in behind her, eager to assist in the frenzied scene. "Gael, please... stop!" Alicia pleaded, her voice a mix of exasperation and concern. "Look what you're doing."

Victoria's cries rose to a piercing crescendo as Gael, still seething with rage, finally loosened his grip. His breath came in ragged gasps as he turned his back on Arnold, who remained frozen, too afraid to move. Gael took a moment to right a toppled chair, using the motion to steady his own turbulent emotions, before planting himself firmly in front of Arnold. His eyes were steely, full of a stern resolve. "How many times have I told you? Be a leader, boy, not a sheep. You hang out with a bunch of punks and soon you become one," he admonished, his voice carrying the weight of both anger and disappointment.

"They're not punks. They're just guys," said Arnold.

"No, maybe you're right. Gangsters is more like it. Yeah, that's it. You're all a bunch of gangsters."

"Don't call me that."

"Then stop acting like one, for Christ's sake."

Alicia saw that Gael's fists were clenching again. "Arnold, go to your room. And Gael, watch your language."

Gael looked at his mother. Once again she saved him from doing something he'd live to regret. Arnold slinked off to his room, thankful for the reprieve.

"Well, he was acting like a gangster."

"I wasn't talking about that," she said, alluding to Gael's use of the Lord's name in vain.

"Oh."

Alicia sent Frankie away, comforted Victoria then threw Gael a roll of paper towels. "*You* made the mess."

Gael took it and soaked up the spilled milk. "Now I have to go into my savings and pay for the damages. My son, a vandal. He was taught better."

Alicia now lent a hand in the clean-up by sponging down the table. "That's what your father and I thought about you sometimes."

Gael filled a bucket of water and grabbed a mop and went at the still sticky floor a second time. "I never did anything like that."

"No, not like that, but there were other things."

Not what Gael wanted to hear right now. Finished with the floor, he next hurled the broken refrigerator magnets into the trash.

"He's a good boy, Gael."

"What kind of good boy vandalizes a school?" He raised his voice, more like a bellow. "Did you hear that, Arnold? What kind of a good boy vandalizes a school?"

Arnold was in his bedroom on the second floor, staring out the window, as he heard his father in the kitchen proclaim, "I'm tired of this. God, I wish Rachel was here. She'd know how to handle him." Arnold spotted the family picture on his desk and punched it. He didn't even notice the pain or blood forming on his knuckles.

"A parent can only do so much," said Alicia. "After that, only time will tell what kind of child you've raised."

"Well, I'm running out of time... and patience," said Gael.

Arnold had heard enough, and the thought of staying in that oppressive house for even one more second was unbearable. He snatched his jacket, flung open the window, and crawled out into the chilly night. He had to stretch himself thin to grasp a nearby tree trunk, then shimmied down its rough bark, feeling the scrape against his skin. As he hurried across the dew-kissed lawn, the echo of his father's booming voice still resonated, driving him into the darkness with a frantic urgency.

Arnold tore through the shadowy streets, his feet pounding the pavement faster and angrier with each step, until the welcoming glow of a convenience store's neon lights appeared up ahead. He slowed to a walk, the adrenaline ebbing slightly, and discreetly wiped the blood from his knuckles onto his shirt tail before tucking it in.

Still simmering with agitation, Arnold fiddled nervously with his jacket zipper as he approached the trio of boys lounging casually against the side of the building. His friend Raul was exhaling a thin stream of smoke from a cigarette, while Spunky and Choo-Choo devoured hotdogs with unrestrained enthusiasm, their laughter mingling with the muffled sounds of the night.

"Hey, how's it hangin?" said Raul. "We thought you wasn't comin'."

"I'm here, ain't I?"

"What's with the attitude, dude?"

"You need to go in and grab a dog," said Spunky.

"So what are we doing?" asked Arnold, impatiently.

"Raul borrowed his dad's car," said Choo-Choo. "We're going to the zoo."

Arnold glanced over at the car, then back at Raul, something not quite sitting right. But he let it go.

"At night?" Arnold glanced at Choo-Choo in disbelief.

"Yeah," said Raul. "We can watch the animals fuck."

Spunky thought about it for a moment then scrunched his face and said, "Shit, they're probably sleepin'."

"Haven't you never heard of night animals? They don't sleep," Raul reminded him. "Arnie's gonna see his first fuck-a-thon."

Arnold flushed then looked at Spunky and Choo-Choo, defensively. "I know how to do it!" Raul sneered while Spunky, his mouth covered in mustard, gave Arnold a couldn't care less shrug.

Just then, a flashy red pick-up truck rolled into a parking spot nearby. Two college-age guys hopped out of the vehicle and strode confidently toward the store entrance. Raul, noticing them, gestured for them to come over and took a few strides in their direction. The young men exchanged a knowing glance, as if anticipating the encounter, and casually approached Raul.

"I got a twenty for you if you buy me a bottle of vodka." Raul whipped out a crumpled twenty dollar bill and a couple of tens. "The big one, right?" he reminded them.

One of the guys took the money with a big smile. "You got it, kid. Always happy to help the less fortunate." The guys entered the store with a chuckle between them.

Raul stood anxiously by the front door, shifting his weight from one foot to the other, eager to get his hands on the forbidden liquid. Meanwhile, his friends remained in place, not wanting to draw any more attention to their illicit endeavor.

Minutes later, the guys emerged from the store, carrying a case of beer and a mini-bar-size vodka bottle, which they playfully tossed to Raul. He snatched it out of the air, but his eyes widened in disbelief as the guys sprinted toward their truck, laughter trailing behind them like a wake. Raul dashed after them, shouting angrily, "What the fuck?! What the fuck?!"

The guy with the beer case tore it open with one swift motion and hurled a can that struck Raul hard on the shoulder. "Consolation prize, loser," he taunted, as the truck roared away, tires screeching against the asphalt. Both guys leaned out of the windows, flipping Raul off with wide grins plastered on their faces.

Fuming, Raul launched the mini vodka bottle at the truck's back window. It spun through the air in a futile arc and landed with a dull thud in the truck bed. "Motherfuckers!" he yelled, his voice a mixture of anger and frustration. He then bent down to retrieve the same can that had bounced off his shoulder, cradling it in his hand as he trudged back to his group. His friends stood in a tense semicircle, eyes fixed on him, afraid to utter a sound.

Raul tossed the can to Spunky who handed it to Choo-Choo. "Let's go... and don't go dripping your shit all over the seats," spewed Raul. Spunky grabbed his two other hotdogs and headed to the car while Choo-Choo added the dented can to his large beer can-filled paper bag. He rushed to keep up. "Yo, back seat, man," Raul called out to Spunky. "And you too, Choo-Choo. Arnie, you're my navigator." They all jumped into the car and Raul peeled out as if he scored a big one.

The backseat boys passed beer cans forward to Raul and Arnold. Raul opened his and the beer squirted out onto the dashboard. "Shit. I told ya to be careful," he shouted.

"You spilled it," said Choo-Choo.

"You shook the can, ass-wipe."

Arnold stayed silent and opened his can extra carefully. The window was rolled down so, between sips, he enjoyed the wind whipping his face.

They passed a convertible with two hot-looking girls in their twenties singing to blasting music. Raul and the backseat boys hooted at them and the girls tried to speed away. But, Raul followed, carelessly weaving through traffic. The girls turned a corner and Raul was right behind them. Arnold was concerned but still kept his mouth shut. The boys then spotted a homeless man walking along the street up ahead, pushing a shopping cart. He heard Raul's car and moved closer to the curb. From the back seat, Spunky leaned forward and grabbed the wheel. "Let's get the bum."

"What are ya crazy from all the shitdogs you've been eatin'?" asked Raul. He then saw Spunky wasn't kidding and took to the idea, wanting some revenge for what happened at the store. "Yeah, let's get the bum."

Arnold gasped. "What?! What are you doing?"

Raul gripped the steering wheel tightly as he directed the car toward the unsuspecting homeless man. The engine's roar grew louder, sending the man scrambling down the street in a desperate attempt to escape. At the very last moment, Raul swerved sharply, the tires screeching in protest. The man stumbled and fell, his cart toppling over with a clatter, scattering its meager contents across the pavement like a burst piñata. Arnold glanced into the side-view mirror, his stomach tightening as he watched the man shaking his fist and hurling curses in their wake. He pressed his lips together and said nothing. A nervous laugh escaped him — thin and hollow, nothing like the gleeful squeals of the others echoing inside the car.

When Raul spotted the girls' car up ahead, he again picked up speed. The backseat boys broke out more beers and when Raul's eyes left the road for a moment, an old lady stepped into a crosswalk. He barreled straight into her. The impact sent her body flying backward onto the curb, where she landed in a crumpled heap. "Holy shit!" he shouted.

"Did you see her fly!" said Choo-Choo.

"Stop the car," screamed Arnold. "We have to go back."

"Fuck that," said Raul. He floored the gas pedal and shot past the girls' car. In a flicker, their eyes met. The eyes of the girls read horror.

"Stop the car, Raul. We have to go back," Arnold said again.

"I ain't goin' to jail for that old lady. She should'na been there."

Arnold's hands clamped onto the steering wheel as he and Raul wrestled for control. The car veered wildly, tossing the boys in the backseat like ragdolls and sending beer cans clattering and rolling across the floor. In a heart-stopping moment, the vehicle tipped onto its side, screeching and sparking as it skidded down the street, leaving a trail of debris in its wake before finally grinding to a halt. Miraculously unscathed, the boys scrambled out of the wreckage, adrenaline coursing through their veins, just as the piercing wail of a police siren echoed through the air and a patrol car rushed up behind them, lights flashing ominously.

The next morning found Alicia back in the kitchen cooking breakfast. At the table, Frankie fiddled with his tablet while Victoria perched her doll at the edge of the table. She moved a tiny plate closer to it.

Gael stepped into the kitchen just as the doorbell echoed through the quiet morning air. He cast a questioning glance at Alicia. "Are we expecting anyone?" he asked, his voice tinged with curiosity and a hint of alarm. The early hour made the prospect of an unannounced visitor even more unsettling. Alicia shook her head, her expression mirroring his confusion. Gael moved towards the front door, his heart beginning to pound with a sense of foreboding. Even through the delicate lace curtains, he could make out the distinct silhouettes of two police officers standing on the porch. A knot of anxiety tightened in his stomach as he reached for the doorknob, bracing himself for the news that awaited them.

"Mr. Fernandez? Do you know where your son is?" asked one of them. It was something no parent wanted to hear.

Alicia suddenly appeared behind Gael, a sense of dread creeping in. "What's wrong?"

"May we come in?"

Gael took a deep breath and opened the door wider to let them in as Alicia, despite all her hand wringing, managed to motion them into the living room. Gael stood with his arms crossed in front of him and his jaw tightened like a bear trap. The one officer then carefully filled them in on the painful details of the night before. With each awful word, both Gael's and his mother's heart sank deeper into despair.

No amount of explaining or excuse-making could extricate Arnold from the tangled web of trouble he found himself in. Gael, his expression cold and unyielding, refused to entertain any of Arnold's pleas or justifications. He explicitly forbade Alicia from intervening or advocating on Arnold's behalf. The decision was final — Arnold was to remain confined in his cold, bleak cell as he awaited the looming specter of his trial. Gael did not visit. He did not call. Whatever words might have passed between them, the silence said enough.

Judgment day came soon to Arnold, though. As Gael stood on the courthouse steps, he peered up at the gray sky, blinking as a mild rain fell against his face. When the door to the courthouse opened, he turned and saw Alicia and Arnold exit. She simply held up her hand with fingers spread, indicating three years. That's the amount of time Arnold would have to stay in a juvenile correctional facility. The others weren't as fortunate; their sentences ranged from five to seven years. When Arnold looked over to his father for forgiveness, Gael simply turned his back to him.

Back at home, Arnold angrily threw a pair of sneakers and some clothes into a duffel bag. He passed his large collection of fidget spinners atop his bureau as he moved to the bathroom where he reached for his toothbrush. It was missing from the holder. He stormed into Frankie's room and found him sitting on the floor looking at his tablet. "You take my toothbrush?"

"No."

"Where is it, Frankie?!"

Frankie looked up innocently. "I don't know."

Arnold stomped out. "Can I have your spinners since you're going to jail?" Frankie called out after him.

Arnold charged into Victoria's room. There on the bed was Victoria with Arnold's toothbrush, using it to brush her doll's hair.

"What the hell are you doing?!" he shouted, his voice echoing through the room. He lunged for the toothbrush, which was hopelessly entangled in the doll's synthetic locks. With a forceful yank, he wrenched it free, tearing out a large clump of glossy hair with it. He flung the tangled mess onto the bed in a fit of frustration, leaving Victoria sobbing as she gazed at her now half-hairless doll, her eyes brimming with tears of despair. Arnold stormed out of the room, his footsteps heavy and his muttered curses echoing in the hallway.

Once back in his own room, Arnold meticulously picked the remaining strands of doll hair from the toothbrush, letting them drift lazily to the floor. He then threw the toothbrush into his open bag with a dismissive flick of his wrist. His gaze soon fell upon his collection of fidget spinners, their vibrant colors gleaming in the light. *Screw Frankie*, he thought defiantly. He gathered them into a haphazard bundle, their metallic surfaces clicking softly against each other, but at the last moment, he hesitated and decided to leave a few behind. Carefully, he wedged the majority into the sides of his duffel bag, ensuring they were tucked away securely, while shoving one into his pocket — just in case he needed its comforting spin later.

Just then, Alicia entered carrying a new toothbrush in its wrapper. Arnold took it then spotted his tearful little sister standing in the doorway looking in. Alicia's stare burned a hole into him. He fished out his old toothbrush and gave it back to Victoria.

Down in the kitchen, Gael sat hunched over the table, meticulously maneuvering a toothpick dipped in glue to coax the doll's unruly hair back into place. His brow furrowed in concentration, but his sighs revealed his mounting exasperation with the delicate task; neither his thick fingers or the hair strands were cooperating. The scent of glue mingled with the robust aroma of percolating coffee. Alicia entered quietly, casting a quick glance at Gael's painstaking progress before moving to the sink. She began to wipe around the faucets, a task more about occupying her restless hands than necessity, her mind drifting as she awaited Arnold's arrival. The silence between them was thick, broken only when Alicia slid a coffee mug over to Gael's side of the table.

In the driveway, the family car stood packed, a testament to the journey that lay ahead. The younger kids were nestled in the back, their faces pressed against the windows, while Arnold occupied the front passenger seat, staring blankly out at the world. Alicia emerged from the house, her footsteps heavy on the gravel, and made her way to the car. She paused, turning back to face Gael, who lingered at the front door with a watchful, forlorn gaze. "Gael, we should all be there for him," she implored, her voice carrying the weight of one last, desperate plea. But her words fell flat, failing to penetrate the barrier of grief and resentment. Gael retreated into the house, the door slamming shut with a resounding finality that echoed through the still morning air. The vandalism, disobedience, and the last straw of vehicular mayhem, were too much for Gael to bear. To him, he had already lost his son. Today, he was burying him.

Alicia got in and started the engine. It turned over a couple of times but the battery died. She stared at the front door of the house. Gael angrily pulled open the door and stood a moment stewing over the situation and the accusatory look coming from his mother. He then grabbed the jumper cables from the back of his pickup truck which was parked right next to her car. Gael popped the hoods and connected the batteries then motioned for Alicia to get out of the car. He got behind the wheel in her place and Arnold immediately left the car and stood a few feet away. He stared off into the distance, not wanting to meet his father's eyes. Gael grit his teeth then turned the ignition key. The engine turned over a couple of times and started. He revved it.

A nosy neighbor, around Alicia's age, stood on her porch, surveying the scene. "It's always something, huh?" she said. Gael revved the engine some more while Alicia's blood boiled as she tried to ignore the woman. "You want me to call Marco? I can call him if you want," the neighbor added.

With the car at a standstill, Frankie jumped out and ran back into the house to use the bathroom.

"No, he's got it, thanks," Alicia told the neighbor. She then poked her head in through the open car window with a worried look.

"It was just sitting too long. It'll be fine," said Gael.

Frankie emerged from the house, zipping up his fly, which cued Victoria that it was her turn. She bolted toward the front door.

The nosy neighbor held open her front door letting the blaring sound of a football game filter out. "Marco, Gael can't get Alicia's car started!"

Gael looked up at the neighbor's house praying Marco wouldn't show.

"Marco!" the woman called out again.

With the engine now running smoothly, Gael waved up at the neighbor and unhooked the jumper cables just as Victoria ran back out and got into the car. Arnold returned to his seat as did Frankie. Gael gave his mother a respectful peck on the cheek. "I have work to do." He went back into the house, avoiding Alicia's and the nosy neighbor's stares.

Arnold watched the front door close. Then he faced forward, hands still, and let the house disappear behind him.

CHAPTER TWO

A GATHERING STORM

Along a stretch of desert road, heat rose in hypnotic waves from asphalt sizzling beneath the midday sun. Alicia's car finally came into view. Arnold, crunched against the window, stared blankly out, still and hollow in a way he'd been since the house disappeared behind him. Victoria slept, sucking her thumb and clutching a blanket and her partially repaired doll, while Frankie hummed softly.

Suddenly, the car hit a bump in the road causing Arnold's head to strike the glass. He looked over at Alicia who was yawning. An instant later, there was a loud pop, signaling a blown tire. The car swerved. "Arnold! Arnold!" Alicia screamed. He grabbed the steering wheel to steady the car as it screeched and skidded.

On the side of the road was a weather-beaten sign: "Welcome to Coyote Junction Pop.18" with a slash through the 18. The car careened right into it and came to a stop with acrid smoke instantly filling the air. Alicia and Arnold got out, coughing, and retrieved the frightened youngsters from the rear. Victoria was crying as she reached back for her doll that was now on the floor while Frankie stood outside hyperventilating. Alicia checked the kids for injuries. "It's okay. We're all okay. Frankie, look at me."

She took a few slow, deep breaths for Frankie to mirror. When he was sufficiently calmed down, she comforted Victoria while Arnold moved off a few paces, scanning the road in both directions and then out into the flat, empty landscape beyond, as if half-expecting something to be there. Alicia then pulled out her cellphone. Useless; there was absolutely no reception no matter which way she turned or how high she held the phone.

Alicia looked at the sign, then up and down the empty road. "Coyote Junction. Bound to have a gas station. Let's go. Arnold, take your sister."

Arnold stood there, staring at the sign as if he were waiting for the population number to change before his eyes.

"Arnold, please!" He shook his head, annoyed at everything, and gave Victoria a little tug before they all headed off down the road while a coyote watched them from a ridge in the distance.

On the porch of a tiny hole-in-the-wall roadhouse-café, Juanita, a fetching 15-year-old in a flowery dress, stood and poured a pan of water onto the wilting greenery. Ruins of old buildings dotted the landscape far behind her while a smaller gas station-garage was off to the side of the house. Juanita looked up and, squinting against the sun, spotted the foursome slowly making their way toward the café. "Papa, hurry," she called out in Spanish. As Alicia and the kids got nearer, the effects of their long walk were apparent. They were sweaty and bedraggled.

Pedro, a man in his forties, Juanita's father, stepped from under an awning where he had been working on a car. "Aiyce. Get some water," he said. Juanita ran into the café, passing the Chief, an ancient American Indian, who sat on the porch in his rocking chair. He looked at the visitors from under his large hat.

"Thank God. I'm ready to drop," said Alicia, as she got to the little building. The family plopped onto the porch steps just as Juanita rushed out juggling a pitcher of water and glasses. She handed out the glasses and began to fill them. When she got to Arnold, she became distracted by him staring at her. The water poured onto his feet instead of into his glass. A pained look of apology fell across her face then she regained her composure and properly filled his glass.

"My, that's good," said Alicia, as she gulped the water. "We blew a tire up the road. Wasn't sure there would even be a town. Where is it anyway?" She looked around.

"Please, everyone, come inside out of the sun." She ushered them in and as the kids entered, they all stared at the Chief as if he were some kind of alien. He stared back until the screen door slammed shut.

Inside, just five tiny tables with the kitchen and a bathroom in back. The café was occupied by the Reverend, a man in his 60s wearing a Reverend's collar and Nathaniel, twenty years his junior who wore a military veteran's cap and a prosthetic leg. They were playing cards at a far table. At another table, a studious looking woman named Margaret, read from a textbook while she nursed an extra large ice tea with two lemon slices perched along the rim. No one seemed particularly interested in the newcomers, although they were surely aware of them.

Juanita pointed to the back. "The bathroom is there."

"Arnold, take the children, please," said Alicia, as she wilted into a chair and fanned herself with a napkin.

While Arnold took the kids to the bathroom, Juanita motioned to her father, who had followed them in, to drag over another table to put beside the one Alicia was at. Pedro quickly brought over the table and Alicia asked him, "Would you be able to get my car?"

"Si. I will go right now. You just rest." Alicia fished through her purse and gave him the keys.

"You must be hungry," said Juanita. "I will make you some lunch."

"Thank you. But, I'm not sure I have enough money on me now with the car and all."

"It's okay. We don't get many people this way. Papa won't mind."

"You're so kind."

Juanita smiled, brought out a basket of tortilla chips, then started preparing a meal. "Now we have some nice company for awhile," she said as she worked.

"It must be fate of some kind. But, I don't think we'll be very good company."

"You been driving long?"

"Yes."

"You have far to go?"

"Have you ever heard of Rancho dos Padres?" Alicia asked.

Just then, Nathaniel slammed his cards onto the table and the men both laughed loudly, distracting Alicia for a moment.

"Si. The camp for boys. Thirty more minutes."

"Thirty minutes? Is that all?" Dismayed, Alicia teared up. "I've been driving as slow as possible." She glanced toward the bathroom and dabbed her eyes with a napkin. "What's it like? Do you know?"

"Hard work. Many boys." Juanita eyed Arnold as he returned with the youngsters.

In what seemed like no time at all, Pedro pulled into the garage, towing the car. Juanita, Alicia and Arnold went out to meet him. The Chief peeked out from under his hat.

"Your wheel rim is bent and the tire is real bad. See?" said Pedro. "I will have to go into the next town to get another one."

"How long?" asked Arnold.

"Maybe three hours. But, I can fix it."

An overheated vintage car now pulled into the road stop. The occupants, Harlan, a tall and lanky middle-aged man and Mimi, an overly large woman with chip-proof makeup, somewhere in her thirties, exited the vehicle and headed straight toward Pedro. Jimbo, whose mammoth size was in direct contrast to his intellect, popped up from the back seat where he was sleeping. He was roughly the same age as Mimi and he followed her and Harlan around like a puppy.

Pedro hopped into his truck. It's not that he didn't notice the new arrival; it's just that he was of the mindset *first things first*. And Alicia was first.

"Hey, where you goin'?" Harlan called out. "I need some oil for my car. She's smokin'."

"I'll be right back," Pedro said, as he drove off. "Wait for me."

"Wait for him? What choice do I have? She's smokin'."

24

Alicia cast a wary glance at the newcomers, silently hoping they wouldn't cause her any trouble. Jimbo had drifted away from the others and stood staring at one of the gas pumps with a fixed, blank expression, as if he were sizing it up, deciding whether or not to take it on in a fight. Feeling a chill despite the warm day, Alicia quickly retreated into the cozy confines of the café, where the aroma of freshly brewed coffee and the soft hum of conversations provided a comforting refuge.

"She's a delicate machine," Harlan continued under his breath. "He better not let anything happen to her or I'll have to hit him one."

"Oh, Harlan, you don't mean that," said Mimi.

"I damn well do mean it."

"Hush. Let's go inside and you can buy us a soda pop."

"Yeah, that'll sure make my day!" Harlan turned toward the café and smacked right into Jimbo who now stood looking at him.

"Hope there's some music in this place," said Mimi. "Come on, Jimbo."

Harlan muttered something unintelligible then headed to the café, followed by Juanita who noticed Arnold staring at the Chief. "That's the Chief," she said.

"What's he the Chief of?"

Juanita shrugged and went back in to continue cooking their meal.

From inside the café, Victoria and Frankie peeked through the window at the Chief and saw Arnold as he walked off toward the gas pumps, kicking the dirt. They rushed out to join him.

"Do you have to go?" asked Frankie.

"I don't want you to go," added Victoria.

"He's making me. I hate him."

"I'm tired," Victoria whined.

"Go sit down if you're tired," said Arnold, especially annoyed.

"But, I wanna go to bed."

"There ain't no bed here, Victoria. You have to go sit down," said Frankie.

Victoria walked back to the porch and sat on a step, head in hands, doll in lap.

"This sucks," said Arnold.

"Grandma said you can't use that word."

Arnold fiddled with the gas pump. "Like I give a shit. I say whatever I want. And I say it sucks."

"Yeah, it sucks."

Arnold smacked Frankie's arm. "Just 'cause I can say it, doesn't mean you can."

"Why can't I say it?"

"'Cause I'm older and I say so."

"Yeah, well one day I'll be older and I'll say what I want."

"Quit crowding me."

Arnold pushed him off and stomped around to the back of the café. As he turned the corner of the building, he spotted a cat grooming itself. He picked up a few pebbles and tossed one at the cat which ran off. Arnold followed it and tossed another pebble that sent the cat hiding in a bush. It was now cornered. Frankie appeared behind Arnold and watched him curiously.

"Come out, come out, kitty, kitty, kitty cat," taunted Arnold. He laughed and raised his hand for another shot.

Suddenly, a large shadow loomed in front of Arnold. He turned around then slowly lowered his hand at the sight of the Chief. Frankie was scared out of his wits and about to run off.

"No, don't run away. You don't have to be afraid," said the Chief.

Suddenly, Victoria turned the corner as the Chief extricated the cat from behind the bush. He pet it gently and as soon as he put it down, it ran into a small shed. The Chief went to the shed and urged the kids to follow. He stood at the entryway as they approached cautiously. Inside, was a cardboard box lined with a towel and filled with four kittens and the mother cat. The Chief gently lifted two kittens, one at a time, and placed them in the hands of the youngest children. He picked up one more and showed it to Arnold. "Now, why would you want to hurt its mother?"

Arnold looked at the frail, trembling animal before shifting his glance to Victoria and Frankie, who were tenderly caressing their tiny, purring kittens. He caught the Chief's piercing gaze, then sprinted away, his heart pounding, until he reached the precipice of a steep cliff. There, he looked out over the vast, sprawling horizon, feeling a mix of frustration and helplessness as he hurled a rock into the abyss and watched it shatter below. Suddenly, a startling sound interrupted the silence — the unmistakable rattle of a snake. He spun around, his eyes widening in alarm as he saw the serpent coiled tightly, ready to strike. Arnold instinctively stepped back, feeling the treacherous edge of the cliff crumble slightly beneath his foot. He froze, his body rigid with fear.

Something drifted to him on the wind — chanting — low and rhythmic, rising and falling with the air itself, a sound he couldn't place or name or find the source of, as if the desert were making it. A coyote emerged, its eyes locked onto the snake. The two animals stood rigid, a tense standoff between predator and prey. The coyote emitted a low, menacing snarl, its hackles raised, and the snake, seemingly sensing defeat, slowly slithered away. The coyote then turned its gaze to Arnold, who was standing there, breathless and paralyzed by fear. With a final, fleeting glance, the coyote darted off, vanishing seamlessly into the vast, untamed landscape as the sound faded with it, swallowed by the whispering wind.

On the porch, the Chief with his hat pulled down over his face, sat and rocked while Victoria and Frankie sat on the lower steps. The sky grew dark as thunderclouds moved in. Arnold approached the Chief. "Are you a real Indian?"

The hat tilted up a smidgen. "I am."

"So where's your tribe?"

Now curious, Frankie and Victoria came up onto the porch and gathered around the Chief. "Long gone," he said.

"Where do you live?" Arnold asked.

"Here."

Arnold glanced at the ruins beyond, trying to figure out why or how anyone could live in this godforsaken place. Victoria pointed to the leather medicine pouch that was around the Chief's neck. "Is that where you keep your marbles?" she asked.

The Chief looked at her for a moment, something softening behind his eyes, then pointed to the side of his head and smiled. "My marbles are up here." He now became serious as he lifted the pouch. "This is where I keep my magic."

"What kind of magic?" Frankie asked.

"Big magic."

The Chief then turned to Arnold. "What is your name?"

"Arnold."

"Hawk," the Chief said with a knowing smile.

Confused, Arnold scowled as Victoria pointed back at the Chief's pouch. "Can I see?"

"Oh no. No one must see another person's magic. It's sacred. Given to me by a great Warrior."

Arnold's interest was piqued but he kept his distance as Frankie sat on a little stool nearby. Victoria closed in on the Chief, resting her hand on his arm, and staring as he fingered the pouch.

"This was the magic that saved the people of this town... when there was a town."

From inside the café, Alicia and Juanita sat sipping their drinks at one table, while Harlan, Mimi, and Jimbo gathered at another. Across the room, the card players leaned in closer, and Margaret paused mid-sentence, all suddenly captivated by the unfolding conversation. Just then, as if on cue from a dramatic play, a bolt of lightning pierced the sky, striking near the ancient ruins of the old town, which seemed to tremble in the oppressive heat. Eyes widened as everyone turned to gaze out the windows. The dry, dusty landscape was alive with tumbleweeds dancing across the ground, and the sky, once bright, now loomed even darker, a brooding canvas of stormy anticipation.

"That was the time the Gangs came to town."

"Gangs?" said Arnold.

"Were they mean?" asked Frankie.

"Meaner than mean. They were devils." Frankie's and Victoria's eyes widened while Arnold's jaw tightened. "But the townsfolk were good people. And so the spirits protected them."

A loud thunderclap sounded and the cat jumped into the Chief's lap, startling the kids.

"There were ghosts?" asked Victoria.

"We call them spirits. My people believe spirits live in many things. Fire, wind, water, the earth…" The Chief began stroking the cat then continued, "even in animals."

Lightning cracked the sky which had now turned a deeper gray. Arnold leaned against the porch railing and the cat's attention was drawn to the sky where, suddenly, a large hawk swooped out of the clouds and veered down toward the road stop.

"And they're always looking for someone. Then they'll get real close to you. And when you're not looking, the animal spirit will grab you and take you on a journey." Victoria gasped and jumped back.

The hawk was now sitting on the rail next to Arnold. It settled its wings with a slow, deliberate fold, and Arnold, without knowing why, shifted slightly where he stood — as if something had changed in the air beside him. No one noticed but the Chief and the cat.

"It's okay. There's nothing to be afraid of. They only look for people who need them and the spirit will always protect you and bring you back home."

The wind howled and dust and tumbleweeds obscured the scenery. A dust funnel formed near the porch and a lightning bolt cut the sky. The rain poured down.

Frankie shivered then said, "Tell us about the magic and the warrior."

"It was a long, long time ago when the town was…" The Chief's voice began to fade, swallowed by the relentless howling of the wind and the drumming rain. Arnold felt a strange sensation creeping over him, an invisible force gently tugging at his very being. Goosebumps prickled across his skin, and the hair on his arms stood upright as if charged by an unseen electricity. His eyes darted around, searching for something he could not see. A chill of fear slithered down his spine. He looked frantically at the Chief, trying to find reassurance in his calm demeanor, then turned his gaze through the window to where Alicia sat, her silhouette blurred and wavering as if the storm had somehow infiltrated the room. Beyond her, Juanita's image began to dissolve, like mist under the morning sun. Suddenly, in a blinding instant, Arnold's *spirit* was swept away, carried aloft by the majestic hawk that soared into the swirling, gray clouds above.

CHAPTER THREE
FIRE AND EXILE

A sudden flash of lightning split the sky, and the hawk veered sharply out of the roiling rain clouds. It soared silently over an American Indian village, shrouded in the inky darkness of night. The bird's silhouette vanished into a swirling, dense cloud of smoke billowing from a burning tipi below.

Pandemonium engulfed the scene. A woman, her deerskin skirt smoldering at the hem, burst out of the fiery tipi, her cries piercing the tumultuous night as she clutched a baby tightly to her chest. Several elders rushed forward, their movements swift and urgent, gently taking the child from her trembling arms and wrapping her fast in a blanket, smothering the ember-glow at her hem before it found its way higher. Meanwhile, other villagers sprinted to and fro, forming a frantic line as they worked together to quench the raging fire consuming the tipi. The air was thick with smoke and the urgency of desperate voices.

After the fire was quelled, a tribesman dragged a young man by the hair and threw him roughly to the ground in front of the burned tipi. He then yanked his head upward, forcing him to behold the destruction and terror he had caused. The young man had Arnold's eyes — that same dark, restless look — but here, in this place and this night, he was Cherokee, and his name was Ahote.

The woman who fled the tipi sprinted up and hurled a handful of fine, gray ashes into Ahote's face, the particles clinging to his skin like a veil of shame. The elders formed a solemn circle around him, their faces etched with disappointment, while the women struck the earth rhythmically with their sticks, creating a resonant, mournful beat that pulsed through the air like the heartbeat of the tribe.

The tribe members parted slowly, creating a narrow path for the Medicine Man to step forward with an air of authority. He reached down, lifting Ahote to his feet with a firm grip, and his voice resonated deeply in the melodic yet stern cadence of the Cherokee language. "Once more, you show no respect," he declared, his words heavy with sorrow and finality. "You have caused much sadness and can no longer be trusted. You are no longer my son. You no longer belong to this tribe, and we are not your people. Go and never return." Ahote stood frozen, his heart pounding in his chest, as if time itself had come to a halt.

The Medicine Man brandished his tomahawk, its polished blade gleaming in the light, a clear and menacing signal. "Go! Go!" he commanded with a voice that brooked no defiance. Ahote shrank back, his eyes pleading silently with those around him, searching the faces of his tribe for a glimmer of mercy or understanding. But the men met his gaze with impassive stares, and the women continued their relentless drumming upon the ground, the sound echoing like a funeral dirge.

With his spirit crushed, the disgraced teen turned away, his head bowed low in resignation and shame. He walked silently into the night, the vast and unforgiving landscape swallowing him whole. As he disappeared into the darkness, he fought to suppress the tears that threatened to spill from his eyes, steeling himself against the rising tide of despair. A coyote's mournful howl pierced the night, a sorrowful echo that seemed to mirror his own inner turmoil.

Hania, adorned with a medicine pouch identical to the Chief's from the road side café, emerged from the throng of men gathered at the tipi. His presence was commanding as he approached the Medicine Man with a purposeful stride. "I will take him," Hania declared, his voice resonating with conviction. "I will teach him respect so that one day he may return to his people."

The Medicine Man regarded him thoughtfully, his brow furrowed. "It is not your place, my brother," he replied, his tone gentle yet firm.

Hania stood his ground, his eyes unwavering. "Our family's blood is strong, and our people need strong warriors," he insisted. "He will learn to tame his wild spirit and come back a man that his father will again want for a son."

From the darkness where he had stopped walking, Ahote turned at the sound of Hania's voice. He knew that voice. Of all the faces in the tribe, his uncle's was one he had never been able to read — but he had always known, in the way you know a thing without being told, that Hania would not let him fall without reaching first.

The Medicine Man pondered Hania's words, the weight of the decision evident in his eyes. After a moment of careful consideration, he nodded, granting his consent.

Ahote's life journey commenced that very same night, under a relentless downpour that drenched the world around him. Hania, draped in a cloak of animal skin, rode ahead on a sturdy horse, his silhouette a dark shadow against the stormy sky. Behind him, Ahote trudged along on foot, the rain soaking him head to toe. His horse, burdened with a travois laden with essential supplies, followed obediently. Together, they navigated the undulating terrain of the hills, their pace dictated by Ahote's ability to keep up, the rhythmic patter of rain their constant companion.

Eventually, they came upon Coyote Junction, a ghost town, eerie even in the daylight. Hoof beats clopped through the mud and rain, moving down the deserted main street.

Ahote's eyes moved over everything — the way a stranger's do, taking quick inventory, filing what might matter. The smell reached him before the buildings did. Woodsmoke and something sweeter underneath it, sugared and fermented, drifting from the downstairs of a hotel-saloon where a woman's scream of cheery delight settled into a raucous cackle and the jangling melody of a honky-tonk piano offered a brittle serenade that filtered through the thunderclaps. Margaret, the same woman from the road stop, now donned in the prim attire of a schoolmarm, discreetly peeked out from the upstairs window, her eyes scanning the scene below.

The piano sounds faded as the Indians passed what was left of the old barber-dentist shop as the Reverend, the road stop card player, with his collar intact, stopped shaving himself to look outside. The streets were rutted deep with old mud, the kind that had been walked and driven through for years. At the jail, an old prospector, Nathaniel from the road stop, sat with his wooden leg propped up in front of the old shell of a building. He was dead asleep, snoring peacefully, entirely unbothered by the rain coming off the eave above him.

The General store was boarded up and further along was the livery stable. The roof of the building was partially collapsed and a lone mule stood in the corral, its head down and shoulders hunched against the rain. The smell here was deep and warm — wet animal and old straw and the faint dark tang of iron from the forge nearby. The blacksmith, Pedro, the mechanic from the road stop, rushed out and gathered up his mule. He stopped just long enough to watch the passersby. His daughter, Juanita, at the side of the building, hurriedly took in the laundry that was hanging on a clothesline, her head down against the rain, the sound of hoofbeats lost in the downpour. Ahote's eyes stayed on her a moment longer than the others.

The Indians kept moving along until finally they came to a small clearing where Hania drew his horse to a halt and declared, "Here."

Ahote's every step had been a struggle against the fatigue that weighed heavily upon him. His clothes clung to his skin, soaked through by a combination of rain and perspiration, and his mood was as dark as the stormy clouds that loomed overhead. Resentment simmered within him, fueled by Hania having ridden comfortably on his horse while he had to endure the arduous trek on foot.

Pausing, Ahote raised his weary eyes to meet Hania's gaze and gestured back toward the town. "So close?" he asked, his voice flat with something that went deeper than exhaustion —— the particular bitterness of a man who has lost everything and is now being told that this is where he starts again.

Hania dismounted and motioned to Ahote to detach the travois. He then walked both horses under a tree where he stood, staring at Ahote, waiting for him to get to work on setting up their camp. Ahote peered up at the gray sky, blinking as the rain fell hard against his face.

By nightfall, while the rain and thunder continued outside, Hania sat in their tipi by the modest fire eating flatbread. Its slightly charred aroma mingled with the earthy scent of the firewood. Ahote sat a bit further away, diligently tending to his weary feet. He smeared a thick ointment over them, then carefully wrapped them with strips of worn cloth, ensuring they were snug and secure. "You haven't told me where we are going," he muttered.

"We are where we are going," replied Hania. "And now we will speak the white man's language."

Ahote looked at his uncle then — really looked, the way you do when you're trying to find the crack in a thing. Hania held his gaze without shifting, without offering anything more. Only his hands moved, turning the flatbread once above the fire, as if the conversation were already settled.

"This is not where I want to live," declared Ahote.

"You will learn to. And so must I."

"You said when we left the village you would teach me the way of the warrior."

"The way of the warrior has many paths. This path leads to knowledge of your enemies. You need to learn more than just his language. You must learn how he thinks. What is in his heart. Just as the deer learns the ways of the mountain lion... to keep from getting killed."

"And if I learn his mind and his heart will I become better because I will have two of each?" Ahote asked with a cocky tone.

"Is one man better than another?"

"Sometimes."

"Is he better because he has more of something?"

"Yes."

"Or is he better because he lives with a willing spirit and a large heart? Is he better because he looks to the spirits for guidance or because he looks to them to find his horse? With guidance he will learn of all the places he may find his horse instead of just the one. Do you understand?" Ahote reflected on his uncle's words, his nod hesitant and uncertain, struggling to fully embrace the weight of the message.

Hania dropped another stick on the fire then wrapped himself in his blanket, lay down and went to sleep. Ahote did the same, though sleep came at him sideways that night, the hard ground pushing against him with a vengeance. When it finally took him, his dreams came vivid and angry — a campfire burning bright with his tribe gathered around it. Ahote and his friend Moki watched from a distance behind a tree. Moki laughed and pointed as the Medicine Man got up to tell a story. "Let's scare them," he said.

"How?" asked Ahote.

"We'll attack the camp and watch the old men cry and fall over trying to run away."

Ahote chuckled in agreement then the two of them sneaked closer to the camp. They wrapped cloth around their arrowheads and struck flints to set them on fire. "Wait. What if we hit something?" asked Ahote.

"A warrior's arrow falls straight and true. I do not miss," declared Moki.

"I am a warrior and my arrow falls straight and true. I do not miss either."

Moki and Ahote rose with their bows and yelled war cries. Moki shot first, sending his arrow into the ground just a few feet short of the Medicine Man. The elders jumped to their feet and the boys laughed resoundingly.

Ahote shouted his war cry even louder as he aimed his bow but paused as if having second thoughts. "Shoot! Shoot!" Moki urged. Ahote's arrow sailed high and far but it hit a tipi. It smoldered and quickly caught on fire. Camp dogs yelped loudly as the Medicine Man turned to see Ahote lower his bow. Their eyes met. The Medicine Man's were filled with anger. Ahote's eyes were filled with fright and shame.

By morning, the storm was gone and the dream was left behind with the dark. But when Ahote rose and moved to the horses, his hands went to work a half-beat before his mind did, fingers finding the familiar task of grooming as if something in him needed the occupation. He relished in the feel of their hides and in their scent as it somehow transported him to a better place and time when he and Moki used to race in the fields near home, jumping over narrow streams and pretending they were great warriors on a hunt.

Hania returned to camp with an armful of firewood. "Today you will scout the white man's town," he said. Ahote now knew better than to question his uncle. He was too tired to hear another lecture so he simply nodded.

The hot sun blazed down upon Ahote as he moved toward town with his bow and quiver. He caught sight of Juanita in a stream, barefoot and frolicking in the water. She was so carefree that he couldn't take his eyes off her. After a few moments, Juanita came out of the water and dried off. She put on her shoes and headed toward town. Ahote followed stealthily.

When she got to the livery stable, Juanita walked up to her father Pedro and spoke to him about something as Ahote strained to hear. He then crept closer and crouched behind a fence as he saw Juanita walk off.

Pedro turned his attention to his mule. He took a wet cloth and wiped her eyes and nose, speaking gently. "You know, my Emmy. You are the prettiest around here." He packed up his tool bag and led her to a little field beyond the hotel-saloon garden. "Of course, your sister Lulu is pretty, too. But, I think it's your ears that make you prettier."

Ahote followed unseen. Pedro let Emmy loose then approached Lulu, his cow. He pulled burrs from her tail and spoke to her tenderly. "I will clean you later, my sweet one." As Pedro walked off, Ahote raised his bow and drew the string back smooth and easy, the arrow finding its line at Pedro's back without effort. He held it there for a moment — long enough to know he could — then let the tension out of the string in one slow breath. The bow lowered. Pedro walked on, unaware, which was exactly the point, and Ahote followed.

Cornstalks swayed gently in the breeze, their rustling leaves harmonizing with the soft, melodic humming of a woman. Nearby, a makeshift wind chime crafted from sticks and delicate shards of glass clinked and tinkled from the branch of an ancient tree, adding a whimsical touch to the pastoral scene. Beside it stood a rustic whiskey still, its copper gleaming faintly in the sunlight, and a small chicken coop bustling with activity, where a proud rooster strutted among his clucking hens.

Margaret carefully filled Juanita's woven basket with an assortment of freshly-picked vegetables, their size and vibrant colors a testament to her green thumb. Ahote, hidden behind a thick bush, couldn't help but let his gaze linger on Juanita as she gracefully carried the basket into the saloon, her silhouette framed by the dappled light filtering through the leaves. She passed by Pedro, who was diligently working to repair the squeaky back door, his hands skilled and steady.

Margaret and Pedro exchanged warm, friendly smiles, a silent acknowledgment of camaraderie as they each busied themselves with their respective tasks. Once Pedro finished his work, he slipped his hammer and nails into the pocket of his well-worn blacksmith's apron, the leather soft and pliant from years of use, and made his way inside the saloon, leaving the sun-drenched yard behind.

Mimi, once the familiar face from the roadside stop, now transformed into a saloon girl with a vibrant, ruffled dress, came bustling out the back door to collect tattered curtains fluttering on a clothesline in the gentle breeze. The sun cast a warm glow on the faded fabric as she hurriedly gathered them.

Meanwhile, Harlan, her irritable yet wise mentor, had taken on the role of barkeeper. He emerged from the dim interior of the saloon to tend to his contraption with a practiced hand. The still, nestled among a clutter of tools and barrels, was his pride and challenge. With a grunt, he nudged aside a small, worn barrel, replacing it with a newer one. When the still sputtered and went silent, he gave it a swift, frustrated kick. "Goddang thing... Ah, there she goes," he muttered, watching the liquid flow resume with relief. "Well, I guess I should be satisfied it's still working at all. Thank you, Pedro!" With a grunt of satisfaction, Harlan hoisted the full barrel onto his shoulder and carried it into the saloon, the door swinging shut behind him, now with merely a muted creak.

The hotel-saloon, that once served as the bustling heart of the town, was the sole establishment that had been maintained, yet it certainly bore the marks of time. The tables and chairs were arranged with precision, creating an inviting and orderly atmosphere, while the entire saloon exuded a warm, homey charm. Wooden stairs, worn smooth by countless footsteps, led up to the rooms on the second floor, each promising a cozy retreat for weary travelers if any ever came.

Ahote peeked in through a side window. He watched as Harlan, at the bar counter, filled bottles with his homemade brew and Mimi and Juanita hanged curtains. Pedro sat at one of the tables with the Reverend, a wealth of knowledge when he was sober.

Suddenly, Mimi rushed over to start the player piano, letting one curtain end drape all over Juanita.

"Not now, Mimi," said Harlan. "It's too hot for music."

"It's never too hot for music. You just tend to your whiskey."

"Miss Mimi, please. I cannot breathe."

"She would strangle my daughter for a song," joked Pedro.

Mimi hurried back and unfurled the curtain as Harlan brought Pedro a glass of water. "You seen them Injuns again?" Harlan asked.

"Not since yesterday. They come for water, though. I can tell."

"Never liked Injuns. Can't trust the sons of bitches."

Juanita scowled at Harlan while the Reverend said, "You never liked anyone, Harlan. Pedro can attest to that."

"Well at least he proved useful. Injuns have no purpose."

"Useful?" declared Pedro. "Maybe I won't be so *useful* next time and you can fix your own damn still."

"Now, now... we all know everyone has a purpose," the Reverend interjected to calm the matter.

"Si, Harlan's purpose is being an ass," offered Pedro.

Mimi cackled loudly and Juanita smiled at her father.

Margaret entered from the back door with a pail full of peas. She put it on the bar and promptly headed upstairs.

"I see Margaret's as talkative as ever," observed the Reverend.

Pedro stared after her. "I've been thinking of asking her to teach me to read."

"What do you need with reading?" Harlan asked with a sneer.

"Can you read?" asked Pedro indignantly.

"Of course I can."

"Well, I should be able to read too."

The Reverend called out, "Mimi, a drink and a song... in whichever order you please."

Pedro finished his water in one gulp then headed to the front door. "I'm going to pick up Nathaniel. Juanita, I did not have time with Lulu today."

"Si, Papa, I will take care of her."

"Watch out them Injuns don't get ya." Pedro ignored Harlan and left.

Juanita left right after him and Ahote watched as she carried heavy buckets of water across the field to a drinking trough for the animals. She was straining under the load. Ahote held back his desire to help her and decided, instead, he was finished with the whole scouting mission for the day, figuring he had better things to do. He moved off, away from the town, and went back to his own campsite and to the chores and activities that awaited him.

Back at the camp, Ahote worked on practicing his hunting skills. He shot an arrow dead center into a gourd that swung from a low tree branch. One arrow was already stuck into it. As he again took aim, Hania, carrying his own bow and quiver, stepped up behind Ahote and made a sound that distracted him. Ahote's arrow missed its mark completely.

"Lose your focus, lose your food," said Hania. They walked together to the gourd for Ahote to retrieve his arrows. "Tell me, what did you learn today from the whites in town?"

"I learned I could kill all of them at any time."

"Then you have learned nothing."

"They are weak."

"Is a man weak because he thinks of other things?"

Hania handed Ahote his arrows then stood with his head directly next to the gourd. "Go back," he instructed. Ahote stepped back but Hania kept motioning for him to move further away until Ahote's back was up against a tree. "There. Now hit the target."

Ahote took a deep breath and aimed at the gourd but lost his focus to his uncle's head. He lowered his bow. "I cannot."

"Because you were thinking of other things."

Hania immediately swung his bow and fired at Ahote, pinning his shirt to the tree. He then walked up to him. "Killing the enemy is easy. Understanding him is hard." He yanked out his arrow, leaving Ahote to rub his arm as if he'd been hit, but he was only gauging the size of the hole left in his shirt. A bead of sweat traced slowly down his brow.

CHAPTER FOUR

SEEDS OF CONNECTION

Pedro pulled up in his creaky, weather-beaten wagon to the mouth of a mine shaft, where the rhythmic clinking of a pickaxe striking rock echoed faintly through the air. "Nathaniel. Nathaniel!" he called out, his voice cutting through the stillness. The metallic clatter continued, now carrying an odd, hurried rhythm that piqued Pedro's curiosity. Urging the wagon forward, he followed the sound, steering it closer to the source — just around to the side, where the landscape was dotted with rugged boulders and strewn with loose gravel. There, beneath the rugged silhouette of the mountains, he spotted Nathaniel, fervently pounding away at the stubborn rocks. Pedro remained up on the wagon, looking down at him. "What the hell are you doing?" he exclaimed, his eyes wide with disbelief.

"I'm building me a house."

"A rock house?"

"Yes siree."

"What's wrong with living in town?"

"Ain't nothing wrong with it. Just always wanted my own place."

"What about food? You cannot eat rocks."

"I'm gonna have Margaret come up here and she can grow me a garden."

"Ah ha! And have you asked her yet?"

"I'll be asking her... maybe... when I'm through building me this house. And I'd be thankful if you didn't bring up the subject of marriage around her. Once you bring it up, it's never forgotten and then they drive ya crazy till ya do it. And, I ain't ready to do it."

"Okay. I won't say a word to Señora Margaret. Not one word."

Nathaniel huffed, grabbed his backpack and climbed aboard. Pedro urged Emmy forward as Nathaniel said, "Don't go getting ideas. I like her is all."

At the Indian campsite, Hania and Ahote were preparing to skin a deer carcass that hung from a tree when they saw Pedro's wagon, in the distance, en route to town. Both parties stared at each other curiously.

"Where the hell they come from?" asked Nathaniel.

"No one knows. Just showed up a few days ago."

"Looks like they're fixin' to stay awhile."

"This is a very big shame. The only horses for miles and they don't wear shoes. I have no good luck."

"Don't worry. One day this town will be hopping again."

As the wagon passed, the deer came into Nathaniel's and Pedro's line of sight. Pedro stopped the wagon and each of them fixated on the deer. Hania noticed their stares and a faint smile crossed his lips. The wagon moved on. "What's Margaret fixin' for dinner?" Nathaniel asked.

"Peas, I think," said a disheartened Pedro.

That night, an oversized bowl of podded peas glistened in the low lantern light of the saloon. The peas were surrounded by dishes filled with hard-boiled eggs, bread and ears of corn. The townspeople sat at the table dead center in the room. Except for Mimi who was at the piano, ready and raring to go. "Lord, we thank you for the food and company. Amen," said the Reverend.

Mimi started the piano then dashed to join them at the table while Harlan poured little shots of whiskey all around, except for Margaret's and Juanita's glasses.

"Nathaniel's building a house," Pedro blurted out with a sudden burst of excitement. Nathaniel, caught off guard, nearly choked on his drink and shot a scowl in Pedro's direction. Pedro merely shrugged, a mischievous grin playing on his lips. Margaret exchanged a knowing look with Nathaniel, whose face turned a deep shade of crimson, like an autumn apple. Meanwhile, Mimi continued to chow down on her meal, completely oblivious to the conversation unfolding around her.

"I don't know why you're still up there, anyway," Harlan interjected with a gruff voice. "Ain't no more gold and you know it." His words hung in the air, thick with skepticism.

Nathaniel straightened up, his eyes gleaming. "Well, you just never know what can happen. A man's gotta follow his dream; otherwise, it ain't worth living," he declared passionately. "Remember that old miner up North I told ya about? Quit working his claim just—"

As if on cue, everyone joined in, finishing the sentence in unison, "five feet short of the mother lode." They all erupted into laughter, the room filled with the warm sound of camaraderie.

After the laughter subsided, Juanita asked, "Señora Margaret, you think maybe you can also teach my Papa to read?" Margaret looked up from her meal. But before she could answer, she noticed everyone looking toward the front door. She turned and saw Ahote and Hania standing just inside. Hania was holding a leather-wrapped parcel. No one dare move. The piano music slowed then came to a stop as if it too recognized this new development. The townspeople looked at one another not knowing what to do.

"Hello," said Juanita.

Hania and Ahote took a couple of steps toward the table but Harlan rose defensively, causing the Indians to stop advancing. Ahote put his hand on his knife and looked at Hania, who met his gaze with a warning. Hania then held his hands out to present his parcel. Margaret motioned them to come forward. "Please," she said.

Hania unveiled his parcel — a large slab of deer meat. "We will trade this." Everyone's eyes grew large at the sight of the meat. Juanita's was more focused on the strapping Ahote.

"For what?" asked Margaret.

"Seeds."

"We have many seeds," said Pedro. Harlan elbowed him. "Well, we do."

"We have seeds in our garden," added Juanita.

Hania put the meat on the next table over. "Good." The Indians stood there quietly waiting for their seeds.

"It's too dark outside now," said Margaret. "I can give you the seeds in the morning. Would that be okay?"

Hania nodded but neither he nor Ahote moved.

"What's wrong with them?" asked Nathaniel innocently.

When Mimi ran over to start the piano again, Harlan screamed, "Mimi! Not now!" The Indians watched Mimi skid to an abrupt halt at the piano.

"Maybe they like some peas," said Pedro. "Hey, you want some peas?" He picked up the bowl. "There's plenty for everyone." Juanita took the bowl from her father and quickly offered it to the Indians. Hania reached in and took some peas then noticed that Ahote seemed mesmerized by Juanita. He elbowed him and motioned him to take some peas. Ahote grabbed a handful.

"Take some corn," said Mimi. "It's good with peas."

The Indians each took an ear of corn and Mimi, without waiting for Harlan's permission, restarted the piano.

"Why don't you pull up a table?" the Reverend suggested.

"Hey, what is this?!"

"Shhh! Harlan, sit down. This is good for relations."

Hania held up his ear of corn, as in thanks, then he and Ahote turned and left the saloon while the raucous piano music played them out.

The next day in the garden behind the saloon, Juanita sat at a small table and practiced her writing while Margaret held up a large picture book for Pedro. Among the books stacked on the table were a worn McGuffey Reader and a couple of other well-thumbed primers alongside the more fanciful volumes. "The whole world opens up for the man who can read and write. There are wonderful stories in these books. Of magic and strange ways of life. Flying carpets and flying horses. Talking bears."

"It sounds like the people who wrote them were drinking a little too much of Harlan's whiskey. Juanita, have you seen these books?"

"Si, Papa. They are wonderful."

"They were written by people with big imaginations and open minds." Margaret then looked up and saw Ahote. "Oh, hello. You've come for the seeds."

Ahote stood near the back door as Margaret went to get the seeds that she had prepared in little cloth packages. He pointed to the vines filled with pea pods. "Yes, they're in there too. Here you go." She handed him the seeds. Juanita broke into a huge smile and Pedro waved good-bye to Ahote, as all of them expected him to leave, but he stayed put, eyeing the books on the table.

Margaret turned back to Pedro. "First, we'll do the letters. The word 'bear'. It's made up of four letters. Juanita, show your father." Juanita wrote the word and held the paper up for Pedro to see then turned it around to show Ahote. Instead of looking at what she wrote, Ahote stretched his neck to see the picture book on the table. "Now you write it," Margaret said to Pedro. Pedro struggled with the pencil in his large hands and looked up several times at Juanita's example.

Out of the corner of her eye, Juanita noticed Ahote's interest in the picture book. Without looking, she slid the book closer to where he was standing. Ahote looked around the table at what each of them was doing, then he opened the book and leafed through the pages. His eyes twinkled at the images then stopped on a page with a picture of a bear. Juanita pointed to the word "bear" under the picture. "Bear," she said.

Ahote looked at Juanita then back to the picture book. "Honaw," he said.

Juanita understood and repeated, "Honaw."

Margaret pulled a stool over to the table and motioned for Ahote to sit. But he chose to remain standing. Juanita held a piece of paper and a pencil out to him. Ahote hesitated so she simply put the paper on the table in front of him and wrote the word "bear". She then pointed to the bear in the book. Ahote finally sat and picked up the pencil awkwardly. Juanita slowly reached over and took his hand. When Ahote instinctively pulled back, she reassured him with a friendly look. He relaxed as she guided his hand. After a moment, Ahote tried to copy the letters. Juanita then turned to her father who had completed his writing of the word "bear". "Look, Señora Margaret, my father wrote 'bear'." Pedro was quite pleased with himself and lifted his paper for all to see.

"Excellent," said Margaret. "And how are you doing, young man?"

Juanita peeked at Ahote's paper. "Si, he has a bear too!"

"Is it better than my bear?"

"Oh, no Papa. But it is very good."

"What is your name, young man?" Margaret asked.

"Ahote," he said, as he looked at Juanita.

"I am Juanita."

"It means God's gift," said her proud father, mostly for Margaret's benefit. "She was, you know."

Margaret smiled pleasantly then turned to Ahote. "Later, I will show you how to write your name."

"Your father will be very proud of you," said Juanita.

"No father."

Who was that man with you?" Pedro asked.

"Hania... uncle."

"I'm sorry to hear about your father," Juanita said, assuming the man was dead. But just hearing the word 'father' had set Ahote on edge. He threw down the pencil and ran off, startling the three of them.

For a moment no one moved, the garden quiet around them, the pencil still rolling where it had fallen. Then Margaret called out, "You forgot your seeds!"

Later that day, Ahote walked through the woods beyond his campsite, carrying his bow and quiver, and still feeling the sting of his encounter with Juanita. He stopped near a pond and picked up a flat stone then skipped it hard across the water. A nearby browsing deer jumped a bit at the sound. Ahote then saw the deer was being stalked by a mountain lion. He aimed his arrow at the big cat and held his breath for a moment. From behind him, a hand grabbed his arrow. The deer ran off as did the cat.

"Were you going to eat the Tsalagi?" Hania asked.

"No. I wanted to kill it."

"A talisman, then?"

"No."

"To kill for food or clothing, yes. To kill for less is not permitted." Ahote remained stoic so Hania asked, "Why do we thank the animal before we take its life?"

"Out of respect for its spirit."

"Respect is also about living in the right way, honoring the earth, the people, and all things." As Hania walked off, Ahote stepped back, right into a snare that sent him aloft, hanging upside-down from a tree. "Perhaps the spirits can help you understand while you hang there."

Back at camp, Hania was gathering brush as Pedro and Margaret drove up in the wagon. She took the seed packages over to him as Pedro stayed put. "The boy forgot to take the seeds," she said.

"I know."

"Where is he?"

"He is off learning to grow."

"He will learn fast, I think."

Hania grunted skeptically, took the seeds, and gestured for Margaret to sit on a tree stump. He handed her a gourd filled with water. "His spirit is troubled and he has much to learn," he said.

Margaret pulled Ahote's writings from her dress pocket and showed it to Hania. "I can teach him some things if you wish."

While Pedro remained on the wagon, his keen eyes detected something amiss with Hania's horse. The animal seemed restless, flicking its foot and pawing at the earth with a certain agitation. Concerned, Pedro approached the horse and discovered what looked like dried mud caked around a concealed wound on its leg. Without hesitation, he returned to his wagon and retrieved a canteen of water and a small bottle filled with a crimson liquid. Carefully, Pedro cleansed the horse's leg, the water washing away the grime to reveal the injury beneath. He then gently applied the red liquid to the wound, watching as it seeped into the cut. Satisfied with his work, Pedro made his way over to Margaret and Hania. "Your horse cut himself. Very dirty. I put some iodine on the cut. Here, you can keep this," he said, handing the bottle to Hania, who accepted it gratefully.

"Well, we'd better get back," said Margaret. "Now, I can expect Ahote every morning?"

Hania nodded and Margaret and Pedro walked to the wagon. "Now you have three students!" Pedro said triumphantly.

"Yes, isn't it wonderful!"

As the wagon headed back to town, Hania went over to check his horse. He sniffed the iodine and was so repulsed by the odor that he again splashed the wound with water then picked up a nearby bowl filled with a poultice. It looked exactly like the mud Pedro just cleaned off. Hania smeared it on his horse's leg, thicker than before.

As the evening sky deepened into shades of indigo, Hania returned to the secluded spot where Ahote was trapped in the snare. The fading light cast long shadows across the forest floor, and the air was cool with the onset of night. Ahote's stomach muscles throbbed with pain, as though a heavy weight had trampled over him, leaving a lingering ache that pulsed with each breath. His repeated attempts to reach up and grasp his ankle, to untangle the stubborn knot of rope, had left him exhausted and sore. Frustration gnawed at him as he recalled dropping his knife after those initial futile attempts, a mistake that now seemed to mock his every effort to free himself.

Hania lifted his nephew onto his shoulder with a firm grip as he carefully untied the snare, making sure it remained mostly intact for future use in trapping food.

Later that night, their horses snorted softly in the cool evening air while Hania and Ahote slept under skins and blankets inside their tipi. But again, Ahote's sleep was troubled. He dreamed of his father, the Medicine Man, now wearing a horrifying mask and coming at him with a tomahawk. The man was shouting and slashing the air before his father's hand rose higher and higher then plummeted downward. It was just about to strike Ahote when he startled awake, sweating. He remained sitting upright, breathing hard, then looked up to the top of the tipi as a hawk shrieked overhead.

In the late morning at the saloon, Nathaniel and the Reverend played cards, as they were accustomed to doing, while Mimi mopped the floor around them and the piano played her favorite tunes. Just as Harlan entered with a barrel of his whiskey, Nathaniel slammed down his cards onto the table. "Ha! Knew you was bluffing!"

Pedro entered carrying an oil can that he put behind the bar.

"Yeah? So how come you're still sweating?" said the Reverend.

"He's sweating because it's hot," said Pedro, offering up his two-cents.

"Harlan, you getting stingy in your old age?" said the Reverend. "More whiskey before I take my business elsewhere."

Harlan laughed loudly at the absurdity of that remark yet poured a couple of drinks. "Yeah, Rev, you just do that."

"Some day," said the Reverend.

"Some day," agreed Nathaniel.

"Yeah, it's always some day," said Pedro, chuckling.

"That reminds me, Pedro, I'm 'bout ready to go back up," said Nathaniel.

"All right. Just so it's before dark."

Nathaniel spotted Margaret coming downstairs with Juanita who was carrying a stack of books. "Say, Margaret, wait up a minute." Juanita proceeded out the back door as Nathaniel went over to Margaret and they went out together.

A moment later, Harlan noticed that Ahote was standing just inside the front door with another leather-wrapped parcel. "Oh, jeez. Can't get rid of him."

Ahote came forward and placed the parcel on the bar. "My uncle said to bring this for the lessons."

"You need lessons about as much as Pedro does. Where do you think it will get you? Huh?"

Mimi scoffed. "Leave the boy alone, Harlan. He's brought us more meat."

"And it goes very well with your whiskey I might add," said the Reverend. "Thank you, son."

Pedro put his arm around the boy's shoulder and led him into the garden even though Ahote twitched from the unfamiliar touch. "You never mind what Harlan says. No one else does."

CHAPTER FIVE
UNINVITED GUESTS

At the mining site, Nathaniel was diligently stacking rocks at the spot where he envisioned his new home taking shape. The sun cast a harsh glare on the barren landscape, illuminating the sweat glistening on his brow. Behind him loomed four formidable figures. Dawson stepped forward first, his steely gaze and rugged demeanor marking him as the one in charge. "Whaddya want?" Nathaniel barked, his voice carrying a sharp edge of defiance, as he swiftly spun around with his double-barreled shotgun.

"You aiming to use that thing?" asked Dawson.

"Depends on what yur doin sneakin' up on me like that. This here's my claim."

"The gold rush is long over, old man. We're looking for Coyote Junction. Ever hear of it?"

"Sure. Whaddya want to go there fer?"

"Where is it?"

Nathaniel showed them the way with the barrel of his shotgun. "Down there 'bout five miles due West. Ain't nothin there, though, 'cept a few good folks and a…"

"There's people livin there?"

"Of course there's people there. It's a town, ain't it?"

Dawson turned to Sully — sharp eyes, strong posture, a woman who missed nothing —her presence beside him as natural and unspoken as a loaded weapon. "Shit. He told me the place was a ghost town."

"So what?" she said. "We'll only be there a coupla days."

"That son-of-a-bitch."

"What's goin on?" Nathaniel asked with growing concern.

"Let's go." Dawson's voice was a low growl as he spun on his heel, taking a few brisk steps before halting abruptly. He pivoted back to Nathaniel, his eyes cold as steel. "You should never point a gun at someone 'less you plan to use it." With blinding speed, Dawson whipped out his Colt 45 and fired a single, deafening shot. The bullet slammed into Nathaniel's wooden leg, splintering it and causing him to crumble to the ground. "And you shouldn't ask so many damn questions," Dawson snarled. Without hesitation, he fired two more shots. Each one drove into Nathaniel's chest and snapped him back hard into the dirt, where he lay still.

Sully snatched up Nathaniel's shotgun, her fingers curling around the familiar cold metal. "Piece of shit isn't even loaded," she muttered with disdain, before tossing it aside with a clatter that echoed in the stillness. She strode over to Nathaniel, her boots crunching against the gravel, and gave him a sharp kick, rolling his limp body onto its back. Bending down, she drew a sharp, gleaming knife from her boot, its edge catching the light as she expertly sliced through the suede pouch hanging from his belt. The pouch fell away, and Sully poured its contents into her palm, watching as the tiny, lustrous pebbles tumbled out. With a sinister laugh, she flung the shiny gravel into the wind, watching it scatter like dust. "Fool's gold for an old fool," she sneered, her voice dripping with contempt. Cracker, a Black man with a sly, cunning grin, watched from nearby, his look one of calculated amusement, while Jimbo — the burly fellow from the roadside stop — sat astride his horse, gripping the reins of the other steeds, his eyes distant as if uncertain whether he truly belonged in this moment.

Meanwhile, in the lush garden tucked behind the saloon, the air was filled with the earthy scent of soil and the faint aroma of herbs. While Harlan was engrossed in the intricate task of adjusting his still, Ahote sat patiently at the wooden table, his eyes keen and expectant for the day's lesson to begin. He observed as Juanita and Margaret moved gracefully among the rows of plants, their hands deftly plucking seeds and herbs, adding to the bounty they had already collected. A gentle breeze rustled the pages of the books stacked neatly on the table, capturing Ahote's curiosity. He reached for a thick, leather-bound medical book and eased it open.

As he slowly flipped through the thick, yellowed pages, he was met with a series of detailed illustrations depicting the human anatomy. Each image was more intricate than the last, revealing the complex web of skeletons, sinewy muscles, and the intricate network of organs that made up the human body. With each turn of the page, a sense of unease settled over him. The illustrations, so precise and lifelike, seemed to leap from the pages. When his gaze fell upon a large, meticulously detailed illustration of an eye socket, its hollow depths staring back at him, Ahote's discomfort turned to revulsion. He leapt to his feet with a sudden jolt, the movement so forceful that his chair toppled over with a loud clatter.

Juanita heard the disturbance and went over to him. She saw the open medical book and Ahote's shock and confusion. He looked at her as if she were a monster. "You skin your own people... for all to see."

She lightly touched his arm, her fingers grazing his skin with the gentleness of a whisper. "Oh no, Ahote. This is a book for healing," she said, her voice soothing yet firm. Ahote's brow furrowed in skepticism and a deeper confusion. "It was written by doctors," she explained. Noticing his puzzled expression, she clarified, "Our medicine men. They look inside us so they understand more. Here, let me show you."

With a graceful motion, she righted Ahote's chair, moving it closer to the sturdy wooden table, and encouraged him to take a seat. He obliged, and she settled beside him, her presence comforting and steady. As she carefully turned the pages, the rustling sound punctuated the quiet of the garden. She pointed out the intricate illustrations of various body parts, the meticulous details capturing the essence of human anatomy.

Stopping on a page that displayed the tendons and muscles of the arm and hand in exquisite detail, Juanita gently traced her finger along Ahote's own tendons and muscles, her touch as light as a feather. She watched intently until she saw the spark of recognition flicker in his eyes. Satisfied, Juanita resumed her journey through the pages, her fingers dancing over the paper until she returned to the page depicting the intricate structure of the eye socket.

Ahote studied the detailed illustration intently as Juanita meticulously pointed out the intricate network of bones, muscles, and ligaments surrounding the eye socket. He gently touched the area around his own eye, his fingers pressing lightly against the skin. "Yes!" she exclaimed, encouraging him.

He experimented by opening and closing his eyes, squinting as he felt the subtle movement of the muscles beneath his fingertips. With a curious mind, Ahote turned another page and was confronted with stark photographs of cadavers, their lifeless forms laid bare for study. "Those people must be very brave," he remarked, his voice tinged with awe.

"What do you mean?" Juanita inquired, her brow furrowing with curiosity.

"It must be very painful," he said softly, still absorbing the images.

"Oh, no, Ahote," she explained gently, "those are people who have passed away.

He stared at the somber photos for a long moment, his mind deep in thought. Then, with a serious expression, he looked her directly in the eyes. "Is that why your people kill so many of mine, so they can look inside to understand us?"

Juanita was totally lost for words, saved only by the sound of piano music wafting out of the saloon as Mimi came dashing out to Harlan. "Harlan, Harlan. Strangers come to town. We got us some customers. Real live customers." Harlan quickly grabbed a whiskey barrel and followed her as she ran back into the saloon to greet the newcomers.

Mimi stood breathless and flushed, waiting at the piano, while Harlan set his barrel down behind the bar with the others, and broke out a fresh bottle. Just as he turned around, the saloon doors swung open, and Dawson, Sully, and Cracker entered, brushing the dust from their travel-worn clothes. "Howdy, folks," Harlan greeted, his gaze sharp and assessing, locking onto Dawson, whom he correctly assumed to be the leader.

The trio sauntered over to the bar, their footsteps thudding against the wooden floor. "Whiskey," Dawson ordered in a voice that brooked no argument. Harlan's eyes gleamed as he skillfully poured the amber liquid into a waiting glass, the rich aroma of his best and only brew filling the air.

Meanwhile, Juanita and Ahote crouched by the back window, their faces barely visible as they peeked through the dusty glass, eager to catch a glimpse of the rugged newcomers.

Harlan's hand then froze mid-pour when his gaze landed on Cracker. His expression hardened, and he spoke with a voice that was cold and unyielding. "I'm afraid I don't serve darkies." His words hung heavy in the air, and Mimi's mouth dropped open in shock.

"Last I heard, they were free men," said Dawson. "Well, maybe I should ask the sheriff."

"Town don't have a sheriff!" Mimi chimed in her usual overly upbeat manner.

"Hmmm, looks like it's five against one," countered Dawson.

"I only see three of ya," Harlan argued.

Just then, Jimbo entered. "He makes five," said Sully.

Juanita gasped at the size of him and took hold of Ahote's hand. Ahote looked over at her, reading the fear in her face as her eyes stayed fixed on Jimbo.

"Hey, Jimbo," said Cracker. "This man here says he don't wanna…"

Harlan quickly poured. "Here's your drink, mister."

"Now, that's more like it," said Cracker, his grin widening as he watched Harlan's hand shaking as he poured both him and Jimbo a drink.

"I guess that'll be eight bits," said Harlan hesitantly.

"We'll be around for a few days," declared Dawson. "So we'll just settle up when we leave. That alright with you?" Harlan nodded his assent as he glanced from one outlaw to the next.

Jimbo started eyeing Mimi with a glimmer in his eye as Sully added, "It makes things simpler."

"Ain't that right, Jimbo?" asked Dawson. "You like things simple, don't ya?"

"Yeah, simple." Jimbo took his drink over to Mimi and Sully watched, amused.

"So where is everybody?" asked Cracker.

"This here's a real small community," said Harlan. "Like you say, it keeps things simple." He then took the bottle off the bar.

"Simple and stupid. Leave the bottle," said Sully. Harlan placed the bottle back in one smooth move, his sigh barely registering with anyone other than himself.

Over by the piano, Jimbo began courting Mimi. "You sure are purty."

"Aw, you're just saying that 'cause you ain't seen a gal in a long time, I bet."

"No, I mean it."

"You like the music?"

"Didn't notice no music."

"You're the sweet one. I can tell."

Jimbo continued his conversation with Mimi while Dawson, Sully, and Cracker settled at a table. Meanwhile, Harlan kept himself occupied behind the bar, pretending to clean up non-existent spills.

"When are they gettin in?" Sully asked Dawson.

"Tomorrow, I figure."

"Sooner the better," said Cracker. "I don't like this place, especially that barkeep."

"It's your smell, Cracker," joked Sully.

"Hey, that ain't nice!" Cracker said, not genuinely offended.

Suddenly, Jimbo and Mimi's laughter echoed through the room, drawing attention as Jimbo exaggeratedly praised her dress and hair, making himself look silly. Sully shouted out to her, "Hey, we all could use a bath. Ya got one?"

"There's a tub upstairs," said Harlan. "Mimi, why don't you fix the er… lady… a bath."

"Sure, Harlan." She then turned to Jimbo. "Now you excuse me, 'cause I have to work now." Mimi then sprang upstairs with a bounce in her step.

"We need some rooms," Dawson demanded.

"With clean sheets," Sully added.

"Shit. I ain't had clean sheets since who knows when," said Cracker.

"I suggest you try a bath first. Otherwise those sheets won't be clean for too long." Sully laughed.

"Go on. Go take your bath," said Dawson. "And don't be long or I'll come get ya."

Sully grabbed her saddlebags and headed upstairs. "The hell you will."

That night at their campsite, Ahote and Hania sat at the fire, cooking and eating. "Some strangers came today," said Ahote.

"I know."

"There's a black man with them."

"I know."

"A woman too."

"I know."

"Why do you think they came?"

"I don't know."

"Do you think they will stay long?"

"I think you should stop asking questions now."

"I was wondering."

"I know. Maybe you should stop wondering."

"I thought you said I must have an open heart and willing spirit to learn many things."

"That is true. But, eat now. Learn later."

Back inside the saloon, Harlan, Mimi, Pedro, Juanita, the Reverend and Margaret all sat at a far table quietly eating dinner, while the gang chowed down at the center table. Jimbo never came up for air.

"Hey, barkeep, another bottle," ordered Dawson.

Harlan jumped up, without waiting to be asked twice, and got more whiskey.

"You got any more of these peas?" asked Sully.

Juanita was about to rise but Mimi, concerned for her safety, stopped her and rushed to get more peas.

"We could use some more of this corn, too," added Cracker.

Pedro whispered to the Reverend, "Where did they come from? Anyone know?"

Harlan returned to the table just as the Reverend answered. "Who cares where they came from just so they go back."

"Hooligans is what they are," said Margaret.

"Shhh! Not so loud," said Pedro. "They might hear you."

Mimi returned after making her delivery to the center table. "What are ya all talking about?"

"Shhh! Not so loud," said Harlan.

"But I didn't say anything."

"Well, keep it that way."

"We're talking about hooligans," said Margaret.

"Gee, I thought the big one was kinda nice."

"You would," said Harlan. "Better just keep your distance 'cause I smell trouble here."

"Me too," said Pedro. "And it stinks."

"Amen to that," said the Reverend. "Harlan, you hear what they're talking about?"

"No, but that darkie was writin' somethin' on a piece of paper and drawing pictures too."

"He can write?" said Pedro, as he stole a peek at Cracker.

"So what are we going to do?" asked the Reverend.

"Nothing we can do… right now," said Harlan. "Just keep our eyes and ears open."

They resumed eating quietly while stealing glances at the gang. Jimbo looked about ready to explode from all the food he was shoveling in. Dawson slammed down his glass. "That's it for me."

"Me too," said Sully, pushing herself away from the table. "I'm heading up to my clean sheets."

"Want some company?" Dawson asked.

Cracker laughed, already knowing the answer. "You ain't the man of my dreams, Dawson." She swung her hips just a bit to irk him as she sauntered upstairs.

CHAPTER SIX

MORE TROUBLE

Hania and Ahote were diligently scraping a deerskin, their hands moving rhythmically as part of the meticulous tanning process. The sound of their tools against the hide filled the air as Juanita approached on her sturdy mule. The sun cast a warm glow over the scene, and as she dismounted gracefully, she and Ahote exchanged warm smiles that spoke volumes. With a picture book tucked under her arm, Juanita walked towards them.

Just as she passed by a towering oak tree, a wasp buzzed aggressively into her path. She instinctively swatted at it, but Ahote's urgent cry of "No!" came too late. Juanita winced as a sharp sting pierced her upper arm, the sudden, searing pain bringing tears to her eyes with the fiery sensation spreading rapidly. Hania made a motion to assist, but paused when Ahote quickly rushed to her side.

Guiding her gently to a nearby fallen log, Ahote knelt beside Juanita, retrieving a small pouch from his belt. The pouch, worn and well-used, contained a healing poultice powder. Through her tears, Juanita watched as Ahote expertly mixed the powder with a little water, creating a soothing paste. As he applied it to her reddened skin, the fiery pain began to ebb away, leaving behind a comforting coolness. Her tears dried, and a grateful smile spread across her face. Ahote handed her the pouch, a silent promise of future protection. "Not for eyes," he cautioned with a gentle smile.

Hania observed the tender interaction between them, a subtle bond forming through shared experience. "Some would say you have learned a painful lesson," remarked Ahote, echoing a familiar piece of wisdom Hania had often shared himself. Hania couldn't help but smile, seeing his own teachings reflected back at him from his perceptive student.

"I shouldn't have swatted at it."

"Everything has a purpose," said Ahote, which left Juanita wondering if she could have just stood still and if the wasp would have gone on its way without inflicting harm.

Outside the weathered saloon, Dawson lounged leisurely, a wisp of smoke curling lazily from the cigarette perched between his lips, his boots propped up on the creaky wooden rail. He exuded an air of indifference, utterly devoid of concern, while beside him, Sully methodically honed her knife blade against a well-worn polishing stone, the rhythmic scraping sound punctuating the stillness. Neither seemed the least bit perturbed by the arrival of a quartet of rough-and-tumble riders. Jackson led the charge, flanked by Billy, Earl, and Leon — each one a middle-aged rogue, their rugged appearances bearing the marks of countless brawls and skirmishes. Their faces wore the hardened expressions of men acquainted with the harshness of life, their bodies scarred from gunfights, knife fights, fistfights, and every other imaginable confrontation. Halting their horses in front of the saloon, they exuded a restless energy, as though searching for something — — anything — to ignite their spirits and stir the simmering tension within.

"Dawson, you comin' peaceful or over a saddle?" said Jackson. He then addressed Sully as if she weren't wearing leather and dirt. "You'd better move away from there, little missy."

Sully stayed put until Dawson flicked his wrist, motioning for her to leave. She ambled to the other side of the door, eyes glued to the other men. Dawson got up slow but ready. "It's gonna take more than you piles of pig shit to bury me."

Just as it looked like they were going to start shooting at one another, a stick of dynamite with a short burning fuse landed in the middle of the riders. Horses spooked and reared. Leon was dumped flat on his back. Billy's horse reared a second time then bolted with him on it.

The dynamite stick was a dud, causing peals of laughter to erupt from Dawson and Sully. Jimbo exited the saloon while Cracker came around the side of the building, lighting a cigar. Both were laughing heartily.

Jackson dismounted, pissed to high heaven. "You stinking piece of shit."

Dawson tossed him a whiskey bottle. "We needed some entertainment around here. Jimbo, take their horses and find that stable man."

"Okay, Dawson."

Dawson led them into the saloon while Sully and Cracker followed in after. Leon kept looking back for Billy but it seemed like he was somewhere off in the hills by then.

Mimi was at her usual chore of sweeping up the place and Harlan immediately hopped to as soon as he saw the new gang.

"Whiskey," demanded Dawson.

"Yes, sir." Harlan quickly broke out the whiskey.

Dawson's eyes narrowed into slits, scanning the room with sharp suspicion. "You notice anything strange going on around here, Jackson?" he asked, his voice low and cautious.

"What do you mean?" Jackson replied, his brow furrowing in confusion.

"Like people?" Sully interjected, her voice cutting through the air like a knife.

"Yeah, now that you mention it. Where the hell did they come from?" Jackson wondered aloud, glancing around at the unfamiliar faces that seemed to have materialized out of thin air.

"That's what we'd like to know," Sully responded, her tone laced with irritation.

"You said you checked the place out."

"They told me it was dead," Jackson protested, a hint of defensiveness creeping into his voice.

"Who the hell are 'they'? *You* were supposed to handle it yourself," Dawson snapped back, his frustration building. He seized the whiskey bottle that Harlan left on the bar and motioned for Jackson to follow him to a table in the corner. The rest of the group stayed clustered at the bar, their eyes fixed on the unfolding scene. "Now, tell me where we're supposed to lay low after we hit the bank," Dawson demanded, his voice a hushed whisper as he leaned in close.

"You want the place dead? It'll be dead." Jackson stood and put his hand on his gun.

"Not yet!"

Dawson sat first and gazed up at Jackson, signaling him to take a seat and shut up for the time being. Harlan dashed over with some glasses.

In the field beyond the saloon, Pedro was cleaning up manure when Jimbo suddenly appeared behind him. "Hey, you, you got more customers."

Juanita came from the chicken coop with a basket of eggs. "More customers!" Pedro declared.

After a while longer, Billy pushed through the swinging doors of the saloon, brushing off the layers of dust that clung to his clothes like a second skin. He looked like he'd been dragged by his horse and was in no mood for anything other than a nice stiff drink. He made a beeline for the bar, where Earl and Leon were already nursing their whiskeys, one after the other. Harlan, standing behind the counter, swiftly poured a glass for Billy, while Mimi diligently worked her way through a mountain of glasses, polishing each one to a sparkling shine. Just then, Juanita came in and placed the basket of eggs on the end of the bar.

At the other end of the room, Sully and Cracker were now sitting together at a table while Dawson and Jackson were still at their own.

Billy said to Earl, "Hey, now what do we got here?"

"Eggs."

Leon and Billy were drooling over Juanita. "To hell with the eggs," said Leon. "There's somethin' better I'm looking at."

"Hey girlie, you fix me up a nice big steak with them eggs," said Earl. "I ain't had a decent meal in a week."

"I'd settle for the girl," said Billy.

"You got that right," said Leon.

Billy crooked a finger to usher her over. "Come 'ere girl."

Mimi immediately pushed Juanita back and Harlan edged closer to her. "We ain't got no steak," Mimi announced.

"Is that right?" said Earl. "I coulda swore I saw a cow when we came ridin' in."

"That's Lulu," said Mimi.

Earl swallowed his drink then sauntered to the back door where he instantly bumped into Ahote as he entered looking for Juanita. Earl pushed him roughly out of the way.

"This town's just fulla interestin' things," said Billy. "Come here, little Injun boy, I wanna see that necklace you're wearing."

Mimi defensively put her hand on Ahote's shoulder. "He ain't hurtin' no one."

Billy's face twisted into a menacing scowl as he glared at Mimi, his eyes dark and unforgiving. With a swift, almost savage motion, he yanked out his gun and gestured violently for Ahote to come over. The air crackled with tension as Ahote and Juanita exchanged anxious, almost desperate glances. Billy's voice rang out again. It was a strange gleeful cackle, like he was playing with them. Then he urged Ahote again, this time with a sweeter tone. "Come on, now, boy. Looks like somethin' my Mama would like."

Ahote stepped forward, his moccasins shuffling against the floorboards, and Billy started fingering the beads. Abruptly, Leon slammed his glass on the bar, demanding another drink. But before Harlan could pour, Leon got up and dragged Juanita over. "Let her pour it."

Juanita, frightened and shaking, poured his drink, keeping her eyes steady on the glass and not allowing herself to become distracted by Leon's rancid breath. Leon then slipped his hand around her waist and pulled her close, his greasy, crusted beard stabbing her neck. Enraged, Ahote charged Leon while Billy was still holding the necklace. It broke and beads scattered across the floor. "No, Ahote!" Juanita shouted, frightened for his safety.

In a split second, Leon spun around and whipped out his gun, aiming it directly at Ahote's head while Billy shouted, "Get back here!" Juanita twisted her body and pulled away, causing Leon's drink to spill onto him and the glass to tumble to the floor. Fueled by rage that mirrored Ahote's, Leon struck Juanita with a vicious slap across her face, drawing a low, pained whimper from her lips, like the sound of a wounded animal. The commotion echoed through the saloon, prompting Margaret to race down the stairs.

Just then, a whiskey bottle flew across the room and shattered against the bar. "Shut the fuck up!" yelled Dawson.

"Make me," said Leon. He then felt a tap on his shoulder and when he turned around, he saw Sully's gun aimed at *his* head.

"I'll make ya," she said.

Leon chortled but still held onto Juanita. "Well lookie here," he sneered, an unusual gleam piercing through the otherwise murky depths of his eyes that locked onto Sully's steely gaze. Without uttering another syllable, Sully pulled back the hammer on her pistol, the metallic click echoing ominously. Leon, feeling the weight of the moment, grudgingly reholstered his weapon, as did Billy, who followed suit. "You're right," Leon conceded, his voice tinged with tension and disdain. "I ain't here for no trouble." He quickly released his grip on Juanita.

Juanita pushed past him and took Ahote toward the back door and whispered. "Go. Please, go!" Ahote glanced over at Sully and saw her determined look. Knowing that Juanita would be safe for now, he turned back to the door. He stood there a moment, his hand flat against the frame, jaw tight — then pushed through it and was gone.

Sully slowly reholstered as she kept her eyes on Leon then turned back and strode to her table. Leon crept up from behind and put Sully in a bear hug. He was squealing with demented laughter until she forcefully threw her head back and CRACK went his nose. His hands flew away from her so he could hold his blood-gushing nose. "Ya fuckin' bitch!"

Leon was doubled over in pain as snotty blood dripped to the floor.

Knowing the average man, demented or not, was no match for Sully, Cracker laughed heartily while Billy's softer laugh was more out of nervousness.

Just then, a gunshot rang out from outside the back of the saloon. Everyone but Leon darted out.

In the field, a wide-grinning Earl, showing off one particularly snaggled tooth, stood over Lulu with his gun still smoking. "Tonight, we got steak!"

Juanita sprinted frantically toward the cow. Margaret arrived a step behind her, and Mimi right after, the three of them converging on Lulu from different directions. Harlan remained frozen, rooted to the spot. Pedro dropped to his knees beside Lulu, gently cradling her head with trembling hands. The Reverend arrived last, breathing hard. For just a moment, everyone was still — the only sound Juanita's ragged breathing and the faint creak of Earl's gun settling.

"Fiends!" bellowed the Reverend, his voice thundering with rage.

"You killed my beautiful Lulu," Pedro cried out, his voice cracking with anguish. "I raised her since she was just a baby." In a surge of fury, he launched himself at Earl, who fired his gun with a deafening crack, the bullet tearing into Pedro's shoulder. Despite the searing pain, Pedro's momentum drove him into Earl, sending them both crashing to the ground in a tangle.

"Papa, papa!" Juanita ran to her father but was unable to do anything amidst the chaos. With one hand, though, Jimbo hoisted Pedro by his belt and lifted him off Earl. Margaret and Mimi grabbed hold of Juanita to keep her from getting hurt.

Juanita's face crumpled as she watched her father hang there, limp and bleeding. Dawson glanced over from the doorway, taking in the scene with flat, unhurried eyes. "'Steaks. Good idea," he said, and turned back toward the saloon. He, Sully and Cracker went back inside while Jimbo stood watching.

Jackson ordered Earl and Billy, "Clean up this mess. I'm gettin' hungry." He too then headed back to the saloon.

The Reverend went over to help Pedro. "Margaret, your handkerchief! We have to stop the bleeding." Margaret rushed over. He took her hand holding the handkerchief and pressed it on the wound. "Keep pressure on it. Harlan, give me a hand." Harlan looked over at Billy and Earl, his body quivering and too scared to do anything but leave. Juanita glanced around for help and zeroed in on Jimbo. He saw her pleading eyes then strode over and delicately scooped up Pedro and took him into the saloon. Margaret hurried along, keeping pressure on the wound.

Ahote, who was hiding behind some trees nearby, saw them taking Pedro inside. He fixated on the dead cow and

Earl and Billy laughing. His hands tightened around his bow until his knuckles went pale, then slowly, deliberately, he lowered it. He turned and moved off through the trees without looking back.

Inside the saloon, Leon sat at the bar holding a bandana to his still bleeding nose and a drink in his other hand. The Dawson gang and Jackson headed to a table while Harlan, knowing his place, hurried behind the bar. The Reverend, Margaret, Mimi and Juanita followed Jimbo carrying Pedro upstairs.

Leon turned to Jackson and sneered, "So what the hell happened?"

"You'd know if you hadn't gotten your ass kicked by a woman."

By the time Ahote reached camp, he was fuming that he couldn't have been more forceful in helping Juanita. He shouted and bashed his hatchet into a log. Hania came in with two dead rabbits and saw that his nephew was too busy being angry to notice. He sneaked up behind Ahote and held a knife to his throat. Startled, Ahote dropped his hatchet. His uncle then released him, stepped back, and gestured toward the log. "What does the log know of your anger?" He turned and dropped the rabbits onto a tree stump while Ahote picked up his hatchet.

"What did you learn today?" Hania asked.

"I learned to hate the white man even more."

"It's not the white man you hate. It's the hate inside you that comes from disgracing yourself, your family and your tribe. And until you face that hate, you will never be a great warrior."

Ahote looked at his uncle, steely-eyed, as he reflected on the events at the saloon. He then asked, "What do I do?"

"Clean the rabbits."

Irritably, Ahote grabbed one of the rabbits, took his knife and was about to slash down when Hania took a cloth and blindfolded him, causing Ahote to immediately stop. He took a moment to calm down then felt around the rabbit to get his bearings. His fingers first touched an eyeball. One finger circled the eye, as if trying to feel the muscles around it. He then ran his fingers down the length of the rabbit, feeling the muscles and intricacies of its body. Now, carefully, through touch alone, Ahote began to prepare the rabbit.

Later, Hania and Ahote enjoyed their meal. "A true warrior must be disciplined and learn to keep a clear head," said Hania. "Only then can you take clear action at the right time." Ahote looked into the fire, as if trying to gain resolve from the flames.

In Margaret's room, the Reverend carefully removed Pedro's shirt. Margaret and Juanita entered with a bowl of water and a stack of towels while Mimi came in with a bottle of whiskey. The Reverend grabbed the whiskey and gulped back a drink before saying, "Pedro, I'm not saying this isn't going to hurt, just see if you can keep the screams down a bit." He then spotted a thin leather book on Margaret's night stand. He slipped it in front of Pedro's mouth. "Bite down on this." He then disinfected a knife and Pedro's wound by splashing on some whiskey. Juanita left the room while the Reverend worked meticulously to remove the bullet, his movements practiced from years tending wounded soldiers during the Civil War. She could hear her father's muffled screams from behind the closed door.

A short time later, Juanita returned with a little bowl of Ahote's poultice paste just as the Reverend was about to bandage the wound. "Wait. This will help." He looked at the poultice suspiciously and sniffed it. "It worked on me," she said assuringly. The Reverend nodded his approval so Juanita dabbed on the poultice then stepped back for him to complete the bandaging.

Pedro slipped into a deep sleep as Juanita continued tending to her father by putting a wet cloth on his forehead and watching his every breath. The Reverend once again swilled from the whiskey bottle to steady his nerves while Margaret hurled the bloody water from the basin out the window and Mimi gathered up the bloody towels and sheets.

A moment later, the door opened and the townsfolk were surprised to see Sully standing there looking in. Sully glanced over to Pedro then over to Juanita. "Any of you sew?" Sully asked.

The ladies looked at one another, curious but frightened. Finally, Mimi nervously said, "I can."

"Good, I need some help." Sully spun around and left and Mimi hurried to follow while looking back at the others who stood wondering what was in store for her. When they got to Sully's room, Sully stood in front of the mirror holding up a picture-perfect schoolmarm's dress with a floral bodice and neat white collar. "Needs fixin'."

"I need to see it on you," Mimi replied.

Sully tossed the dress on the bed then unbuttoned her vest and took it off while Mimi watched with awe. She'd never seen a female gunslinger before, let alone one who was getting undressed before her very eyes. But that's as far as Sully went; she slipped the dress on over her other clothes. "It's too big."

"Sure is purty, though." Mimi sized up the chore facing her, first carefully eying the dress, then Sully then back again to the dress. "I guess I can put some tucks in here under the arms and in the waist. That outta help some."

"Okay, do it."

"You know, I could fix your hair," Mimi offered politely. "I mean if you want me to."

Sully checked herself in the mirror. "What would ya do to it?"

Mimi gently took hold of Sully's long hair. "Well, I can put it up like this." As she held the hair up, she noticed scars on the back of Sully's neck. Sully quickly pulled away, causing Mimi to let go of her hair. "Or maybe you'd like a braid." She twisted Sully's hair in a loose makeshift braid.

"Yeah, that's kinda nice," said Sully, genuinely pleased. "What do you think?"

"Purty."

The two women looked at each other in the mirror for a moment, something passing between them that neither one named.

From behind them, came Leon's obnoxious, raspy voice. "Yeah, real purty."

Sully caught sight of him in the mirror as he stood in the doorway. "A peach and a plum, all ripe for the pickin'," he said. Sully walked to the door and kicked it shut. Leon turned and stood with his back to the door, grinning, and a wisp of drool exited his lips.

The next day, a tiny pebble hit Margaret's window. She peered out and spotted Ahote motioning in the direction of the mule and wagon that was waiting further back. Margaret went downstairs, a shawl draped over her shoulders. The Jackson gang members, who were gathered for a meal and a planning session, noticed but said nothing.

"Mimi, I need to get some herbs for Pedro. Could you please go up and watch him for me?"

"Sure, Miss Margaret. Is he awake for some food yet?"

"I don't think he feels like eating but I'm going to make some tea." Margaret whispered something to Mimi before heading out the back door. She slipped off to the garden where she met Ahote, and they walked to the wagon and drove off.

By now, it was late afternoon when the wagon approached Nathaniel's mine site where Hania stood with his horse near the entrance. Ahote stopped the wagon and Margaret spotted Nathaniel's body. She jumped off and ran to him. "Oh, no. Nathaniel!" She was crying as she tried to move closer to the body but Hania put his arm out to stop her. She cupped her hand over her mouth against the stench of a person long dead.

"I saw the vultures." He pointed to where vultures sat on rocks and on the ground and watched from a distance.

Margaret took her shawl and held it out for Hania who draped it over Nathaniel's body. "I will burn his body and offer it to the spirits for safekeeping."

"No, please. That is not our way. He should be buried."

Hania realized that the customs of the white man differed significantly from those of the Indians. With Ahote's assistance, he set to work digging a grave, choosing a spot nestled between the yawning entrance of the mine and the place where Nathaniel had begun building his home. They understood well that the grave needed to be deep, ensuring that the earth would rest undisturbed, protecting the body from scavenging animals that prowled the wilderness.

The sun dipped below the horizon, casting a warm, golden glow across the sky as Margaret knelt beside Nathaniel's grave. The air was still, and a gentle breeze rustled the leaves of nearby trees. The Indians stood quietly a short distance away, their presence respectful and solemn. Margaret reached into her pocket, her fingers brushing against the smooth seeds she had brought with her. She carefully scattered them over the grave, each seed a silent promise of life and remembrance. With a deep breath, she rose, her shadow stretching long across the ground as the last light of day faded away.

"We must get Juanita away," said Ahote.

"She won't leave without her father and he can't be moved." Margaret looked back down at the grave. "I have to get back before they miss me."

"She is right," said Hania. "We must gather our thoughts."

Margaret got into the wagon where she clasped Nathaniel's backpack against her chest. It was now all she had left of him. Ahote jumped aboard and drove the wagon away as Hania followed on horseback.

CHAPTER SEVEN
DOUBLE JEOPARDY

In the dimly lit saloon, Earl and Billy sat at a battered wooden table near a front window, nursing their drinks. The air was thick with the scent of stale tobacco and spilled whiskey. Earl casually glanced outside and noticed a bustle of activity at the livery stable, where the weathered wagon had just rolled to a stop. "Looks like our little Injun's back," he remarked.

Billy followed Earl's gaze and saw Margaret deftly unhitching the tired mule while Ahote swiftly mounted the back of Hania's sturdy, chestnut horse. The horse's coat gleamed in the moonlight as it shifted impatiently. "And he brung a big Injun with him," Billy noted, his voice tinged with disdain.

As Hania's horse trotted off with a steady rhythm, kicking up small clouds of dust in its wake, Earl leaned back in his chair, a sly grin spreading across his face. "We outta teach that redskin a lesson," he suggested, his tone dripping with malice.

"Or two," Billy added, a dark glint in his eyes as he drained the last of his drink.

Margaret quietly entered the saloon from the back door and joined Harlan, Mimi and the Reverend who were sitting having dinner.

"She sure took a long time to get those herbs," said Billy.

Margaret leaned in close, her voice a soft murmur as she shared her news with the townsfolk. Their eyes widened, and they struggled to mask their shock and disgust from the prying eyes of the lurking gangs. Mimi, her heart heavy, was particularly moved by the gravity of the situation. She wrapped a comforting arm around Margaret, guiding her gently up the creaking wooden stairs. Margaret's tears, glistening like tiny crystals in the dim light, began to cascade down her cheeks once more, leaving a trail of sorrow in their wake. The Reverend softly mumbled a prayer for his dear friend while the others bowed their heads in remembrance.

Leon was at the bar swilling whiskey while Jimbo sat at his own table stuffing himself with meat. Earl then whispered something to Billy. After a moment, they pulled up chairs to sit with Jimbo. "Hey, Jim-Bob," spouted Earl. "Steak's good, ain't it?"

"It's Jim-bo! Jim-BOW."

"Oh, sorry, Jim-BOW. Hey… Billy and me saw two Injuns dropping off that old lady before. Well, we snuk up on them 'cause well, we thought maybe they was gonna hurt her, and guess what we heard they was sayin?"

"What?" Jimbo asked between forkfuls, only vaguely curious.

"The big Injun said he was gonna come back here late tonight and kidnap your girl Mimi. Ain't that right, Earl?"

"That's right, Billy."

Jimbo's brow furrowed as he tried to picture Mimi being carted off against her will.

"Said he was gonna take her back to his tipi and make her his squaw."

"Nah. She wouldn't let him," Jimbo protested.

"We ain't kiddin', Jimbo. Now ain't that the most disgustin' thing you ever heard?" Earl dug at him. "An Injun takin' a white woman away from her home."

"And what do ya think he's gonna be doing with her in his tipi?" Billy taunted. Jimbo became real concerned now. He downright stopped eating.

Earl answered for him. "Gonna force her to make little half-breed Injun babies."

"That's right, Jimbo," said Billy. "They do that ya know."

"Ain't he got an Injun woman of his own?"

"Shit, yeah, but they don't care," said Earl. "They're not like you and me and ole Billy here."

"They'll do whatever they can to make us mad. You know that." Billy winked at Earl.

"Now all we wanna know is, whaddya gonna do about it, eh, Jimbo?" Earl asked.

Jimbo threw down his fork causing a wad of fat to go flying. "I'm gonna git him."

Hania and Ahote were sitting by their campfire talking when Earl, Billy and Jimbo, on horseback and out of hearing distance, surveyed the scene.

"Now, you know what to do, don't ya, Jimbo?" asked Earl.

"I'm gonna git him."

Earl and Billy smiled as they raised their rifles and aimed at the campfire. They fired off a number of rounds which sent embers flying up into the Indians. The gang immediately took off toward the camp.

Ahote was suddenly engulfed in a shower of burning embers, sparks catching in his hair and searing his exposed skin, the smell of scorched flesh sharp in the air. The Indians' horses bolted in panic, prompting Earl to fire a shot, killing Ahote's horse but missing the other. With urgency, Hania grabbed a blanket and hurled it over Ahote, desperate to smother the flames. The rowdies dismounted swiftly, encircling Hania with menacing intent. Jimbo lunged at him, knocking him to the ground, and unleashed a barrage of relentless, brutal punches into his face and chest.

Billy seized Ahote, who was writhing in agony from his burns, and delivered several vicious blows to his head, while Earl goaded Jimbo on with cruel enthusiasm. Hania let out a primal howl, summoning every ounce of strength to break free. Ahote, fueled by sheer desperation, fought off Billy and leaped onto Jimbo's back. In one swift motion, Jimbo halted his assault on Hania just long enough to violently hurl Ahote off, sending his head crashing into a heavy rock.

With Hania reeling, Earl swung his rifle butt with devastating force, rendering him unconscious. As Hania lay motionless, Billy mercilessly drove his boot into Ahote's ribs, eliciting a sickening crack. As Jimbo glanced at Ahote's battered body, he barked, "That's enough."

"No, it ain't enough," Earl retorted viciously.

"I got him like I said I was gonna git him. He ain't gonna be coming after my Mimi now." With a grim, satisfied nod, Jimbo mounted his horse and galloped off.

Earl's voice rang out with fury, echoing across the open landscape. "You chicken shit, fat, coward," he yelled, his words sharp and biting. Billy, standing beside the flickering flames, gestured toward the fire with a mischievous glint in his eye. "Hey, Earl," he called out, his tone suggesting a plan.

"Good idea," Earl responded with a wicked grin. Together, they approached the tipi, its canvas sides billowing gently in the night breeze, and set it ablaze. The flames licked hungrily upwards, casting a sinister glow against the dark sky. Mounting their horses with a sense of triumph, Earl shouted into the night, "Sleep good, red bastards," his voice dripping with malice. With a cacophony of whoops and hollers, they galloped away, the sound of their chaotic laughter lingering in the air long after they had vanished into the darkness.

Ahote lay semi-conscious on the ground facing the burning campfire and tipi behind it. His eyes opened slowly then he blinked and focused on Hania.

Soon, the tipi was reduced to nothing but a smoldering pile of ashes, its smoky remnants curling up into the sky. Hania lay wrapped snugly in a woven blanket, his face weary yet serene, as Ahote sat beside him, carefully lifting a wooden bowl to his lips to give him water. "I feel like an old woman," Hania remarked with a wry smile, his voice a raspy echo of its former strength.

Ahote looked at him with admiration. "When the elders spoke about the great warriors," he began, his tone reverent and filled with pride, "it was always of Hania they spoke. Of you, my uncle. They told tales of the spirits bestowing their magic upon you, to guide us and shield us from harm."

"The spirits are saving you for something special too, Ahote," Hania replied, his words weighted with conviction and a hint of mystery.

"I don't know what to do," Ahote confessed, his voice barely a whisper, as uncertainty clouded his mind.

"A true warrior dares to do the impossible," Hania encouraged, his gaze steady and unwavering.

Ahote lowered his head, his confidence wavering. In that moment, he did not feel the spirit of a warrior; doubt clung to him like a shadow, making him question if he would ever rise to such a challenge.

"Put your faith in the spirits, and you will know what to do," Hania advised, his voice a gentle command wrapped in wisdom. With a laborious effort, he reached for his medicine pouch, the worn leather soft beneath his fingers, and draped it around Ahote's neck. "What was given to me by the spirits is now given to you. To protect and guide you on the path that lies ahead."

The air seemed to hold its breath as Ahote absorbed the weight of his uncle's words and the significance of the pouch now resting against his chest. His hand came up slowly and closed around the pouch, his eyes down, feeling the pull of it — and everything it carried.

A moment later, with Hania's encouragement echoing in his ears like a sacred chant, Ahote kneeled beside his dead horse. He stroked its sleek mane, feeling the warmth of the animal beneath his fingers, and then his eyes shifted, lingering on the distant horizon where the town lay waiting.

A candle flickered atop a table cluttered with dirty dishes as Dawson's gruff voice broke the silence. "Get this shit outta here," he commanded. Mimi hurried over to where Dawson, Jackson, Sully, and Cracker were seated and swiftly tidied the table.

After Mimi left, Cracker spread out a piece of paper with a drawing on it. Dawson pointed to it, tapping once with his finger. "The bank's here and here's where they got the safe. We break through from the dress shop next door."

"Then, Cracker blows the safe," said Sully. "We'll be gone before anyone can get to us."

"And what are my boys doing while you're in there with the cash?" Jackson asked.

"Keepin' the rest of 'em busy with a little fireworks here and there," Dawson explained.

"Fireworks? And she says no one's gonna notice?"

Dawson flicked at the paper, irritated. "This isn't some small town bank. This is a city bank and it's fulla railroad money."

"How much ya figure?"

"Over a hundred and eighty thousand dollars," said Sully.

"Oh, sweet Jesus!" Jackson exclaimed, leaning back in his chair, genuinely amazed by the total amount. He then squinted at Sully before turning his attention back to Dawson. "Okay, what do we do?"

"The night we break through, you and your men are going to light up the sheriff's office. They'll be too busy putting out the fire."

"Then what the hell do we need her for?" asked Jackson.

"I'll be there a day before you guys arrive to tuck the old lady away and set up shop."

The piano was still tinkling away. Leon was at a table with a half-empty whiskey bottle as Earl and Billy entered laughing. They went straight over to him. "Leon, you shoulda seen it. It was something," said Earl.

"What the hell you talking about?"

"We taught them Injuns a lesson. Right, Billy?"

"We sure did, Earl."

Earl picked up Leon's whiskey bottle and took a swill. He then passed it to Billy, who also took a drink before returning it to Leon. Leon, meanwhile, was preoccupied with watching Juanita as she moved across the room and went upstairs with a basin of water.

"Hey, Leon, what's the matter with you?" Billy said.

"Nothin'."

Leon grabbed the whiskey bottle and headed upstairs, sliding his hand along the banister to keep steady.

"Wonder what crawled up his ass," remarked Earl with a scowl.

Leon staggered down the dimly lit hallway, his footsteps echoing against the worn floorboards as he approached Sully's room. He paused in front of the door, his gaze fixed on it for a moment, before his fingers fumbled with the buckle of his belt. Just then, the creak of a door opening broke the silence, and Juanita emerged from Margaret's room, her arms laden with fresh towels, their clean scent faintly perfuming the air. Leon, with a sudden burst of energy, lunged toward her, his movements swift and predatory. Startled, Juanita turned, her eyes wide with alarm, and attempted to retreat back into the safety of Margaret's room. But the door seemed impossibly far, and she couldn't reach it in time. Leon clamped his hand over her mouth, silencing her before she could cry out, and dragged her swiftly down the hallway, his grip unyielding. They disappeared into the shadows of the dark, unlit room next to Sully's, the door closing behind them with a quiet, ominous click.

Inside the bedroom, faint moonlight shined in through the window. "One sound and I'll fucking kill your papa and all your friends." He threw his gun belt onto the bed, not noticing that it had no mattress until it clunked against the wooden slats. Still, it wasn't loud enough to have been heard downstairs. He set his whiskey bottle on a nightstand and pushed Juanita up against the wall, tearing at her clothes.

Juanita was crying and pushing against him. When he started to undo his pants, Juanita's hysteria escalated and she tried her best to fight him off as he slobbered all over her.

Sully, clad in a nightshirt haphazardly tucked into her pants, burst through the door with a gun firmly in hand. The room, previously shrouded in shadows, was now further illuminated by the hallway light. She quickly assessed the situation as Leon swung Juanita around to shield himself. Sully's gaze darted to Leon's gun belt lying nearby. She quickly snatched it up and slung it over her shoulder. Her voice was steady and commanding as she aimed her weapon at Leon, "Let her go, asshole."

"What's it to you?"

"I said let her go... now."

"Okay, okay." Leon pushed Juanita toward Sully. He then grabbed the whiskey bottle, threw it, and hit Sully in the head. She was knocked to the floor, dazed, and dropped her gun. Leon grabbed Juanita by the hair and threw her back into a far corner. He then pushed the door closed and kicked Sully's gun under the bed. He stepped toward her menacingly. "You don't look too comfortable laying there. Let me help ya up." He kicked her in the stomach. "Yur not so tough now, are ya, bitch?" He kicked her again. Sully moaned and appeared unconscious.

Leon looked over to Juanita who was huddled in the corner, fumbling to pull something from her pocket. He grinned viciously and moved to her and, just as he reached down to grab her, Juanita flung the open pouch of poultice into his eyes. He balked, screamed in pain and stumbled backward.

Sully came to and reached for her boot knife. She drove the razor-sharp blade into the top of Leon's foot. His screams bounced off the walls as he dropped to his knees. Sully yanked the knife out and thrust it under his chin. "Get up," she ordered.

Leon struggled to his feet, his movements sluggish and pained, while Sully swiftly maneuvered behind him. She shoved him toward the door, propelling him out onto the balcony. The men inside the saloon, engrossed in their drinks and chatter and being serenaded by cheery piano music, were abruptly alerted by the sounds of scuffling and Leon's pained moans. Their heads snapped upward just in time to witness Sully, her expression cold and unyielding, draw a blade across Leon's throat, the gleam of metal catching the light. With a swift push, she sent him over the rail. His body pitched forward and dropped hard, hitting the wooden floor below with a sickening thud. "Jackson, get this piece of shit of yours outta here," Sully commanded with icy detachment. She turned and retreated to her room, while Juanita stood frozen, her eyes fixed on the lifeless form sprawled below.

"I told ya to keep your boys in line," said Dawson.

"Jackass. He never could stop fucking with the women."

CHAPTER EIGHT
TWISTS OF FATE

In the field beyond the garden, Earl and Billy alternated digging Leon's grave. Sweat was beading on their foreheads and their shirts were taking on a new layer of stain and stench. Jackson was at the back door of the saloon watching the digging while the Reverend was at the bar drinking, knowing they'd come looking for him before too long.

Jimbo sat at a table, watching as Cracker meticulously cut fuses with precision and inserted them into sticks of dynamite. The gritty surface was littered with scraps of fuse and dust, a testament to their careful yet hazardous work. Cracker, with his calloused hands, passed each prepared stick to Jimbo, who gingerly placed them into an open wooden crate on the floor beside him. The morning sun poured through the window, casting a warm glow that highlighted the crate's contents and gleamed ominously off the dynamite's surface.

Cracker noticed the sunlight creeping over the explosives and frowned, his voice gruff with concern. "Look, if you wanna learn about dynamite, you gotta listen. I told you, don't let the dynamite sweat. Keep it out of the goddamn sun."

Jimbo, his face a mix of confusion and worry, replied, "You told me not to sweat when I'm holding the dynamite."

With a sigh of disbelief, Cracker shook his head, his patience thinning. He swiftly moved the crate out of the sun's reach and extracted a stick of dynamite, examining it closely. A few glistening beads of nitroglycerin clung to its surface like dew on a leaf. Cracker swiped a bead off with his finger and flicked it across the room. It detonated with a sharp crack, a tiny explosion that sent a shockwave of panic through the room, causing everyone to jump in their seats.

Jackson, startled by the sudden noise, spun around, his hand instinctively reaching for his gun, eyes fixed on Cracker.

Cracker, unfazed, held up the stick of dynamite as if to make a point. "Yeah. Let's all go up together."

Jackson, realizing the situation, slowly reholstered his weapon, his eyes still wary. Cracker turned back to Jimbo, who was visibly trembling, his face pale as if he might be sick at any moment. "You see what I'm talking about?" Cracker asked, his voice steady but firm.

Jimbo nodded, swallowing hard, clearly shaken by the close call, understanding now the gravity of their work.

Dawson and Sully descended the stairs, with Sully carrying her saddlebags. "What the hell was that?" Dawson inquired.

"Just Jimbo learning what *not* to do," said Cracker.

Billy entered from the back door. "We're ready out here. Any of you wanna pay yur respects to Leon?"

"How's this for respect?" Sully spit on the floor. Jackson headed out while Jimbo looked over at Dawson.

"Go ahead. Sully and me got some final business before she leaves." Jimbo got up and left the saloon, happy for the reprieve from things that go boom.

"I'll be right back," said Cracker, who disappeared through the front door with the fully stacked box of dynamite.

"Hey, Rev, ya coming or what?" asked Billy. The Reverend swallowed his drink then headed out after Billy.

In the field, the men all took their places at the grave with the Reverend at the head of it. He solemnly removed his hat just as Billy and Earl hurled Leon's body into the deep hole. "Let's make this quick," said Jackson.

"Here, Lord, lies one of your minions by the name of?" The Reverend looked over to the men.

"Leon," said Earl.

"Ah, Leon what?"

"Just Leon," said an already impatient Jackson who started tapping his foot against the ground.

Earl suddenly heard an odd sound high in the sky and looked up.

"Here lies Leon. May he rest in... may he just rest. So sayeth the Lord. Amen," the Reverend finished and donned his hat.

THUNK! An arrow landed right in the center of Earl's chest. The men scattered and took cover except for Billy who slipped and fell into the grave. The smell was overpowering, and the thought of his situation filled him with revulsion, yet he was too scared to climb out. More arrows rained down on them so Billy stood on Leon's body and joined Jackson in firing blindly. Leon's bloated carcass released a final gush of putrid gas that only added to Billy's dismay.

Meanwhile, at the front of the saloon, Sully was on horseback and Dawson was strapping on another saddlebag. They turned in the direction of the gunshots. "Wait here," said Dawson, as he ran into the saloon.

Out in the field, Jackson hid behind a barrel while others hid behind trees. Jackson motioned to Billy and Jimbo. "Get the horses and head them off." Billy stuck his arm straight up out of the grave and Jimbo, without breaking his stride, hoisted Billy out. The Reverend, meanwhile, made a mad dash back to the saloon.

Dawson crossed the floor of the saloon to the back door just as the Reverend ran in and upstairs. Jackson came running in too. "What's the shootin' for?" asked Dawson.

"Injuns got Earl. Headed this way."

Dawson went back out the front door with Jackson following. A moment later, Jimbo and Billy rode up with Billy holding the reins to Jackson's horse.

Bewildered, Sully asked, "What the hell's goin' on?"

"Injuns comin'," said Billy. He threw the reins to Jackson who rode off around the other side of the saloon. Jimbo and Billy then rode off in different directions.

"Sully, get back in there," ordered Dawson. Sully dismounted and grabbed her rifle. "You see any Indians, you shoot 'em," he said, as she rushed inside.

Cracker came running up. "Injuns?"

"Get your rifle and meet me back here," said Dawson.

"I got a better idea." Cracker ran off in yet another direction.

The townspeople were now gathering anxiously on the balcony, their faces a mix of curiosity and fear. A few began to trickle downstairs but Sully was right there brandishing her rifle at them. "Get in one of those rooms and stay out of the way. I don't wanna hear a peep out of any of ya," she barked, her voice sharp and commanding.

Meanwhile, Billy, perched atop his restless horse, navigated the narrow, shadowy alleyway, his eyes scanning the surroundings for any signs of Indians. Just then, Ahote sprang from the corner, a sudden blur of movement that caught Billy's attention. With a swift maneuver, Ahote retreated back, leading Billy to give chase. As Billy rounded the corner, Ahote charged forward, waving a sack that flapped wildly in the air. Startled, Billy's horse reared, its whinny piercing the air as Billy tumbled unceremoniously to the ground.

Scrambling to his feet, Billy's hand flew to his gun, his finger fumbling for the trigger. But Ahote was quicker, his movements fluid and precise. With a deft flick of his wrist, he hurled a knife that sailed through the air with deadly accuracy, embedding itself in Billy's gut. A pained gasp escaped Billy's lips as he squeezed the trigger, the bullet burrowing uselessly into the dirt as he collapsed, the world spinning around him.

Cracker, now carrying a pouch with sticks of dynamite on his belt, moved past the livery. He was unaware that the pouch flap was covering all but one stick of dynamite that was sweating from the sun. He heard a sound coming from a nearby shed. "That you, Jimbo? Dawson? Jackson? Anybody in there?" He broke into a huge grin, and without looking, grabbed the sweaty stick of dynamite. While his other hand reached for a match, a bead of nitroglycerin on the stick he was holding dripped down into the pouch.

BOOM! Cracker blew up. Bits of him scattered the landscape.

From the saloon, Sully heard the explosion and ran out the front door while Ahote came in unnoticed through the back door and sneaked upstairs.

Inside Margaret's room, the townspeople stood uneasily at the foot of the bed. Juanita sat, out of view, on the side of the bed where Pedro rested. Ahote entered and frantically looked around. "Juanita?"

The townspeople parted and Juanita rushed into Ahote's arms. "I'm scared," she whispered.

"What can we do to help?" asked Harlan. The others appeared taken aback by his question. "This is my town too!" he declared.

Sully was now at the front of the saloon peeking through the doors when Ahote, on the balcony, purposely made a noise. She turned, looked up and spotted him running down the hall. Sully tore upstairs and just as she passed Margaret's room, the door opened and the townspeople descended on her like a pack of coyotes. Ahote then stepped in, took Sully's guns and handed them to Harlan.

Back around the livery stable, Dawson stood looking at what was left of Cracker just as Jackson rode up. "Did Cracker get him?" He then spotted a few chunks of Cracker's fingers. "Son-of-a-bitch. Billy's dead too."

"I'm gonna make sure it takes those bastards a long time to die," muttered Dawson.

"This ain't gettin' us nowhere," reasoned Jackson. "They're pickin' us off one by one."

"I'll find Jimbo, if he's still alive, and meet ya back at the saloon."

Ahote was dashing out the back door when he bumped right into Jackson who walloped him in the face then dragged him inside while taking his weapons. The gunslinger then dragged Ahote to a window where he ripped off a curtain cord as he looked around curiously and wondered aloud, "Where the hell is everyone?"

Upstairs, Harlan heard the thud of Ahote hitting the floor and the scrape of boots dragging across the wood below. He stood very still for a moment, listening, then picked up one of Sully's guns and moved down the hallway.

As Jackson began to tie Ahote to a post, Harlan appeared at the top of the stairs with the gun pointed at Jackson's back. "Let the boy go," Harlan demanded. Jackson, sensing a gun on him, stopped what he was doing and raised one hand in surrender while spinning around with his own gun drawn. He and Harlan emptied their guns at each other. Jackson was hit and fell to the floor dead, having caught one in the throat, as Harlan tumbled into a still heap at the bottom of the stairs. In a flurry, Ahote untied himself, grabbed his weapons and ran out the back door.

Dawson was almost at the front of the saloon when Jimbo rode up. "Have you seen any of 'em?" Dawson asked. Jimbo shook his head 'no' just as an arrow struck him deep in his thigh. His horse bolted and Jimbo hit the ground hard. Dazed, he crawled over to the porch. Dawson looked up and fired repeatedly at Ahote who was now down the street. Ahote ran into an alley.

Dawson then saw Juanita through the saloon window kneeling over Harlan's body. He rushed in, grabbed her and dragged her outside while putting a gun to her head. "Come out Injuns or I'll kill the girl." Juanita struggled in his grasp. "Come out where I can see ya or I'll kill her right now." He cocked the hammer. After a moment, Ahote walked into the middle of the street. "Drop the bow and come closer." Ahote took a dozen steps closer. "Where are the others?" Dawson asked. Ahote raised his head high and smiled devilishly. "You gotta be kiddin'," said Dawson. He fired a shot that knocked Ahote to the ground where he lay motionless, his face in the dirt.

Dawson shoved Juanita over to Jimbo for safekeeping. She noticed the arrow in Jimbo's leg and the blood dripping onto the porch. They looked at each other, both recognizing the fear in each other's eyes. Dawson then cautiously approached Ahote. As he stood over him, he said, "You dirty little bastard." He reholstered his gun and pulled out his Bowie knife. "I'm gonna carve you up." He then kicked Ahote over onto his back and saw a long graze wound at the top of his forehead.

As Dawson bent down, Ahote used his leg forcefully to sweep him to the ground, catching Dawson completely off guard. Dawson's knife flew out of his hand and landed a few feet away. They both scrambled to their feet. And while Ahote drew his own knife, Dawson drew his gun. He pulled the trigger without hesitation. CLICK. Dawson was out of ammo. He responded with a fierce throw of his hefty weapon at Ahote, the impact smashing into the boy's shoulder with a thud. Dawson swiftly snatched up his knife, and the two began a deadly dance, circling each other with predatory precision, their blades cutting through the air in a vicious symphony, each slash an attempt to draw blood. Ahote's heart pounded like a war drum, and he felt the blood surging with relentless force through his veins.

Dawson saw an opening that allowed him to grab a hold of Ahote's wrist but Ahote quickly returned the favor. Despite the lock, the much bigger and more experienced Dawson overpowered him. He slammed Ahote against the hitching rail and pounded Ahote's knife hand against it until the knife dropped. He kicked it away then grabbed Ahote's hair and pulled his head back hard. Dawson put his own knife to Ahote's throat. "Your kind thinks it'd be honorable to die fighting," Dawson sneered. He then unexpectedly re-sheathed his knife. "But to be beaten to death like some mangy dog in the street." He closed his massive hand into a fist and punched Ahote hard in the face, knocking him to his knees. As he raised his fist to slam him again — WHOOSH. An arrow struck Dawson in the back of his shoulder. He turned to see Hania galloping up on horseback.

Ahote recovered enough to grab Dawson's Bowie knife from his sheath and thrust it into him, twisting it deeply inside the older man's gut with both horror and satisfaction. Fully exhausted from his effort, Ahote then fell back away from the body.

Hania, still fragile and recovering from his harrowing ordeal, carefully dismounted his horse as Juanita dashed over to Ahote. Together, they gently helped Ahote to his feet, their movements tender yet urgent. Hania's gaze then shifted to Jimbo, who sat slumped on the porch, his face a mask of pain and resignation. With deliberate slowness, Hania approached him, his fingers wrapping around the hilt of his knife. "No, please don't hurt him," pleaded Juanita, her voice a mix of desperation and concern. Hania paused, glancing at Ahote, who silently shook his head, signaling his disapproval. Despite the silent plea, Hania continued his approach toward Jimbo. He lifted his knife, poised to act, but instead of a vicious strike, he brought it down to sever the arrowhead. The metallic clink echoed as the arrowhead fell to the wooden floorboards of the porch. With a steady hand, Hania then pulled the long, slender shaft of the arrow out through the opposite side of Jimbo's leg.

Juanita burst back into the saloon, her heart pounding as she darted past the lifeless forms of Jackson and Harlan, their bodies sprawled on the floor. She raced up the creaking stairs with Ahote close behind, the air thick with tension. Flinging open the door, her eyes fell upon Sully, bound and gagged on the floor, with Mimi perched triumphantly atop her. Juanita hurried to her father, her voice steady yet tinged with emotion. "It's over," she declared, as tears trickled down her cheeks.

Ahote stepped into the room, his presence commanding a shared sigh of relief from the townspeople gathered there. He guided them downstairs, leading Sully, whose hands were securely tied, ensuring no further harm could be done. As they descended, Mimi's gaze landed on Harlan's motionless body, a gasp escaping her lips as she rushed to his side. Meanwhile, Juanita enveloped her father in a protective embrace.

"Harlan? Harlan? Say something," Mimi said, as she frantically searched Harlan's body. "I can't find no holes!" Suddenly, Harlan moaned and his eyes fluttered a bit. "Miss Margaret, you got any of those smelling salts of yours?" Margaret hurried back up the stairs to her room.

Mimi gently cradled Harlan's head in her lap, softly caressing his forehead as he began to regain consciousness. "Wha...what happened?" he asked, his head throbbing violently.

"I guess you fell and hit your head," she replied. "You did really good, Harlan," Mimi assured him. Harlan shifted his gaze and noticed Jackson's lifeless form.

"Well, I guess I did at that."

Hania entered the saloon with Jimbo in tow. Mimi promptly let go of Harlan's head, causing it to hit the floor. "Ouch!" he exclaimed, rubbing the back of his head.

She ran to Jimbo and helped him to a chair then looked at Hania and smiled in thanks for not killing her true love.

Harlan struggled to his feet, still massaging his head, as Margaret descended the stairs with a peculiar expression, carrying the salts in one hand and a sizable leather pouch in the other.

"What's wrong, Margaret?" asked the Reverend.

She held up the pouch. "It's Nathaniel's. It was in his pack." When she reached the bottom of the stairs, she opened the pouch and removed several half-inch size gold nuggets that she held up for all to see.

"Guess there was some gold left up there after all," Harlan said.

Pedro added, "He said he didn't want anyone to know until his house was finished. A big surprise, he said, to share with all his friends. It's yours now, Señora Margaret. Nathaniel was building that house for you."

"Well I'll be damned," said Harlan. "Then the fools gold he carried was just for claim jumpers. They'd think he was just a crazy old man." Sully shook her head and let out a half-hearted chuckle as she was reminded of her own reaction to Nathaniel's fake gold dust.

"You were all Nathaniel's friends," said Margaret. "It belongs to everyone. Even you, Mr. Hania... and Ahote, of course."

"Our people have no use for your yellow stones," Hania responded.

Margaret placed her hand on Ahote's shoulder. "If you want this boy to have an education, like I think you do, then you're going to need it."

Hania contemplated Margaret's words then said, "Before he takes that path, there is still another he must follow. I will bring him back when he is ready."

Harlan turned toward Sully. "What are we gonna do about her... and the big guy?"

Jimbo sat up nervously, his eyes darting around as if searching for reassurance, while Mimi gently placed a hand on his shoulder, attempting to soothe his frayed nerves. The Reverend walked over and stood before Sully, his presence commanding the attention of everyone gathered. "I've been away from the good book for quite some time," he began, his voice steady yet carrying the weight of his conviction, "but as I remember, it says to turn the other cheek." His gaze then swept over the others, addressing them with a calm yet firm tone. "If they promise to go far away and never return, can we let them go?" The townsfolk hesitated, their faces a tapestry of emotions; brows furrowed in contemplation, and jaws set in reluctant determination. The Reverend then turned his focus back to Sully, his eyes filled with a blend of sternness and empathy. "Young lady, of all the things you might be capable of doing," he continued, his voice laced with a hint of admiration for her grit, "and I would bet you're probably pretty darn resourceful, it might behoove you to find a new career." His words hung in the air, a gentle yet firm suggestion laced with the hope of redemption and new beginnings.

Harlan then added, "Something a little more lady-like."

"Or blacksmith," said Pedro. "You'd probably make a good blacksmith. Strong arms."

"Maybe we should just let her go find her own way," suggested Margaret.

The Reverend cut her loose and Sully walked over to Jimbo. "Come on, Jimbo, let's get out of here."

Jimbo looked helplessly at Mimi. "I'd kinda like to stay."

"What do ya all think?" said Mimi to her fellow residents. "I'd like him to stay."

After mulling it over, the townspeople registered their consent with thoughtful nods.

"Okay, Jimbo, you stay here if you like," said Sully. "I guess you always needed a better family than we ever were to you." She patted him on the arm then headed for the door. She slowed her step just before she reached it, half turning as if something had pulled at her — then she walked on. "Take care of yourself."

"Bye, Sully," said Jimbo sadly. Mimi gave him a big kiss and he hugged her back.

Ahote looked longingly back at Juanita as he and Hania left the saloon but he believed in his uncle's promise that one day he would come back.

The sun rose over the remains of the Indian camp. Ahote sat quietly by the fire as Hania approached with a piece of bread in one hand and a lump of charcoal in another. He held them out for Ahote to choose. Ahote selected the charcoal. As Hania watched, Ahote spread the charcoal over his face and arms. He then rose and they walked to a little clearing by a thicket of trees beyond the camp.

Both Indians took their hatchets and chopped branches to fashion a small shelter. When completed, Ahote took his place under it. He stuck his knife in the ground in front of him and Hania left without a word.

Throughout the week, from dusk to dawn and back to day and night, Ahote endured the elements. He shivered and waited, slept restlessly, and huddled against the relentless rain. He chanted, feeling weak, exhausted, and hungry. On the final night, he awoke to see the full moon reflecting off his knife.

The moon's reflection diffused to become white smoke wafting upward from the knife and, from the smoke came a standing bear, closer and closer. It roared several times then raised its massive paw with long sharp claws as if to strike. The bear then morphed into Ahote's father, the Medicine Man, who gently placed his hand on Ahote's head. "A man becomes a true warrior only when his heart is more powerful than his anger." Ahote's vision quest ended and he now slept peacefully.

That night, the trees swayed gently and the sky twinkled with millions of stars. From a nearby hill, Hania, on horseback, took his last look at Ahote and rode off.

The brilliant white glow of the moon shifted into a blazing yellow sun, casting a warm, golden hue over the landscape. A majestic hawk glided gracefully across the sky, its wings spread wide, spiraling down toward the earth with an effortless elegance. As the hawk descended, the deep, resonant voice of the Chief at the roadside café echoed, "And Ahote learned the path he would follow and soon he became a man."

The Chief sat on the porch in his timeworn rocking chair, its wood creaking softly with each gentle sway. Victoria, nestled comfortably in his lap, listened intently to his words. At the Chief's feet, Frankie sat cross-legged, his eyes wide with wonder. Nearby, Arnold leaned against the weathered porch post, his eyes on the Chief with a quietness in them that hadn't been there before.

"So, Ahote forgave his Daddy with the help of the spirits?" Frankie asked. The Chief nodded then looked at Arnold. "So what happened to Ahote?" said Frankie.

"First he learned how to be strong in spirit and heart... not just in body. Because that is the way of our people. Like his father, the Medicine Man, he became a healer. Ahote studied very hard and became the first of his kind to graduate from medical school. He became a doctor to his people."

"I like that story," said Victoria. "You have any more?" The Chief's eyes twinkled in delight and he laughed softly.

At the open window of the café, Juanita cleared the table. "Every time I hear that story, it gets better."

"He has such a colorful imagination," said Alicia.

Pedro exited the garage and called out. "Señora Fernandez. Your car is ready!"

Alicia came outside and settled up with Pedro while, back at the porch, the kids got ready to leave.

"Did the little Indian boy give you the magic bag?" Victoria asked.

"Come on, children," said Alicia. "Time to go." Alicia went to the car and the children followed as Juanita exited the café with a lunch bag.

Victoria waved at the Chief. "If you see the little Indian boy, tell him I said hi."

"I will," assured the Chief.

Pedro and Juanita stood at the driver's side of the car talking to Alicia. "Thank you for everything," Alicia said.

Juanita handed her the bag. "He didn't eat much," she remarked, glancing at Arnold, who was now seated in the back with Victoria. She smiled as Arnold met her gaze, his eyes softening.

"Be careful you don't fall into no more holes," said Pedro.

Arnold's window was rolled down and the Chief approached the car. He opened his medicine pouch and pulled out a small piece of amethyst crystal that he placed in Arnold's hand. "What was given to me by the spirits is now given to you. To protect and guide you in the path that lies ahead." He closed Arnold's fingers around the crystal. "The warrior is strong in spirit and heart. Because without that, the magic cannot work." He stepped back away from the car as Alicia started the engine. Harlan, Mimi, Jimbo, Nathaniel, the Reverend and Margaret had all come out of the café to bid their farewells, and the car pulled out amid waves and smiles.

Arnold glanced down at the crystal then looked out the back window to see the Chief remove his hat and wave. He noticed the deep three-inch scar at the top of the Chief's forehead — and his hand closed tighter around the crystal.

The car traveled a short distance and passed another old weather-beaten sign: "You Are Now Leaving Coyote Junction. Come Again."

THE END

AUTHORS

 Ginger Marin is an actor, author, screenwriter, environmentalist and animal rights advocate. As a former network TV Journalist at NBC News NY, Ginger served as producer and writer for the network's top news shows and various special reports. Ginger is also the author of "Monster on Mars" and "Adventures in Avalon: An Offbeat & Quirky Adult Bedtime Story". To learn more about Ginger's acting and film projects, visit her IMDB page at http://www.imdb.me/gingermarin or her personal website https://gingermarin.com. If you want to read how she bemoans the world, check out her blog at http://bioniclady.com

J Bartell, M.A., is an author, screenwriter, and behavior specialist, renowned for developing and teaching his process known as 'Left-Right Brain Suggestibility.' He was previously a licensed Marriage, Family, and Child Counselor in California. In his mid-thirties, J became Chief of Staff at one of the world's largest therapeutic/educational institutes. At that time, he gave lectures and live demonstrations of Pain, Bleeding, and Muscle Control at UCLA and other venues. His clients included people from all walks of life, but it was his worldwide travels on behalf of affluent, private individuals, including heads-of-state, that put him on the radar of the CIA. For more information about J, visit his website at http://jbartell.com.